THE LITTLE WASHINGTONS:
FARMERS

"DID YOU EVER RIDE A COW?" ASKED JOHN.

The Little Washingtons : Farmers.   *Frontispiece.*

THE LITTLE WASHINGTONS: FARMERS

BY

LILLIAN ELIZABETH ROY

Author of

THE POLLY BREWSTER BOOKS
THE LITTLE WASHINGTONS BOOKS
GIRL SCOUT SERIES, ETC.

ILLUSTRATED

NEW YORK

GROSSET & DUNLAP

PUBLISHERS

Made in the United States of America

CONTENTS

CHAPTER   PAGE

   I. MR. VERNON'S FRIENDSHIP . . . 7

  II. HORSES FOR THE ARMY 22

 III. NEW IDEAS FROM THE BOOK . . . 35

 IV. WASHINGTON'S FISHING GAME . . 51

  V. READING NEW GAMES 71

 VI. LITTLE WASHINGTONS' FOX-HUNTING . 85

VII. SHALL WE PLAY SHEEP OR SLAVES? . . 104

VIII. THE WANDERERS FOUND 125

THE LITTLE WASHINGTONS: FARMERS

CHAPTER I

MR. VERNON'S FRIENDSHIP

"THERE'S Mr. Vernon, just going into that shed," said George Washington Parke, as he with his three playmates ran across the back lawn of the farmhouse called "Woodlawn," in Vermont.

"You coo-coee to him, George, and let him know we are coming," advised Martha, too breathless to call or whistle for herself.

Instantly three boys' voices shrilled: "Coo-oo-eee! Mr. V-e-rr-n-n-on! Wait a minute."

In another instant after that a white-haired head was seen in the doorway of the shed and the children felt relieved.

"The rain is over for the day, isn't it?" said Martha, the moment they had greeted the smiling old man.

"So it seems," returned he, looking up at the scudding clouds overhead.

"And we thought it might be as well if we-all took a walk across the field, to visit John's future home. You promised us you'd tell us how it came to be known as 'Vernon Home Farm,'" was George's polite reminder to this new friend.

Mr. Vernon smiled and said, "So I did. Well, does your mother think it dry enough to cross the field? Of course there is a wide footpath straight across, but the ground may be damp."

"Oh, we never bother about wet shoes or damp feet. Lots of times down home we keep right on playing, after one of General Washington's battles ends with us in the brook; or Jim, there, all wet and covered with mud-cannon balls. They are the only kind we can shoot, you see,—not being allowed to use guns or arrows," explained John.

Mr. Vernon laughed heartily and agreed that mud-shot was safer than lead bullets.

"I've been thinking over this rainy day, wondering what you could find to pass the time. Had I known you were longing for some fun, I could have invited you to the hayloft and told you a fine story about Colonial Days, when my great-great-grandfather lived in Lexington."

"Oh! do tell us now, Mr. Vernon," begged Martha.

"We'd just as lief hear about *that*, as to cross that wet field to visit John's house," added George.

"Yes, because I s'pose we really ought to wait for our folks to accompany us," was John's thoughtful reply, showing how willing he was to give up such a treat for the sake of sharing it with his parents.

Mr. Vernon smiled, but said nothing to this sudden change of plans. Then he looked at Jim—the little colored boy who always played the games of Little Washingtons with the three white comrades.

"And what do you want to do, sonny? Hear a story, or go see Vernon Homestead?" asked the old man.

"I'se ain't pertickler. What Marfa and th' boys like, I gen'ally likes, too," returned Jim.

"Then we'll climb up to the hayloft and hear about the times when Paul Revere took that famous midnight ride, and when all the American Rebels—as England termed them then—realized that a real war was at hand before they could call themselves free."

"Wow!" exulted George, winking his eyes at his friends.

"Just what we want most of all—a story of the Revolution," added Martha.

"And think of it," laughed John, "your folks and my folks were so relieved to find we brought no Washington books of battles. Then, right here ready-made for our game, we find the best kind of book—one who can tell us all the new stories from his own family history."

"Don't let's lose a word of what Mr. Vernon tells us, 'cause we can remember them all next winter when we are home once more," advised Martha.

Mr. Vernon was not aware at that time that these Little Washingtons used the stories of the Revolutionary War and General Washington's part in it for games, which they played by acting the battles and sieges too literally for the peace of their families' minds.

Having seated themselves comfortably in the large light hayloft, the children were ready for the tale. They had taken a swift survey of the loft, and each one felt sure that it would lend itself beautifully for a game at some future day. Since the same conclusion had been reached by each one of the four, they were now waiting to have Mr. Vernon begin his narrative.

"I see you like this hayloft, eh?" chuckled the old man. "Well, so long as it isn't filled with new hay, you are welcome to play up here. I know how fine these haylofts are for children to play in."

The Little Washingtons grinned and thought their host a most understanding man. They felt sure that he understood children.

"Now to start my story: My ancestor, as I told you, lived on a small farm near Lexington. He made a business of raising horses, which at that time were in great demand and brought high prices. Every one had to plant their own gardens, and many had farms. Oxen were used for plowing and heavy cartage, but horses were preferred, when they could be had,—and when the buyers had the price to pay for them.

"I suppose you know all about the Boston Tea Party and the matters which actually led up to a break with the Old Country?"

The children quickly said that they knew all that, so Mr. Vernon proceeded.

"Grandpop Vernon, as he was called by his friends, was heart and soul with the Revolutionists, and he not only enlisted his sons to fight, but he wanted to go, too. He was too old and crippled with rheumatism to be of any service fighting, so he stayed at home and raised horses for the armies.

"In the first outfitting of the raw recruits of farmers of Massachusetts, my grandsire furnished more than twenty horses. He kept enough only for breeding purposes for the future need of Washington's men; and not only horses, but food and clothing and whatever was needed by the soldiers. He had an old smithy on his farm near the road which ran to Boston, and in this smithy he hammered out many a bullet and steel weapon to use to carry on the warfare for freedom.

"Well, one day a fugitive rushed into the shop and begged for refuge from the British squad which had found him on duty as a spy upon their movements. Grandpop Vernon bethought himself quickly, and no spot could he think of but the great furnace which was used when he was at work with anvil and bellows. It chanced this day that there was no fire in it because he had other important duties to perform, and, being a thrifty man, he had allowed the fire to go out.

"In a moment, therefore, he had hurried the fugitive over to the big fire-pot and had thrust him inside the empty pit. None too soon, either! He had scarcely reached his anvil once more where he was hammering away with cold irons, when the handful of British rode up and dismounted before his low shop door.

"Then a cross-fire of questions and answers began, all of which could be heard by the young chap hiding in the furnace. The British went about the little shop seeking for the escaped spy, and Grandpop Vernon seemed quite indifferent to them. He sauntered over before the furnace door, and took hold of the handle on the bellows. This he started to pump, whistling the while, to impress the British with his desire to go on with his work.

"One of the Redcoats started to open the furnace door; but a soldier on guard

out in front of the shop, now warning
those within that a suspicious cloud of
dust seemed not a mile down the road,
turned the British from their quest. In
a moment, they were in the saddles and
were fleeing from the place.

"Five minutes after that the comrades
of the man in the furnace rode up and
asked where the Redcoats had gone.
Then the fugitive came from the fire-
pit and thanked his savior. His horse
had been shot down under him, so
Grandpop Vernon fitted him out with
another mount and saddle and sent him
on his way with his blessings."

Mr. Vernon was cajoled into telling
other stories of his grandsire's part in
the Revolution and the Little Washingtons heard more details and thrilling
escapes of those who fought under their
great General's command, than they
had ever read of in the books.

Every time Mr. Vernon finished one
story the children began clamoring for
another; and so it went, until the sounds
of many voices near the back porch
informed the Little Washingtons that

Pete and the servants had arrived in the automobile. To his relief, Mr. Vernon then gladly excused the four children and they ran down from the hayloft to see what was the news from Pete.

Now that the servants had arrived for the Graham family no excuse could be had to keep John from going with his parents to the Vernon Homestead. The field-path had dried completely, so the Parke family decided to accompany their friends across the meadow to their new summer home. Mr. Vernon had preceded them, with Pete and the servants in the car.

Not one word of Mr. Vernon's tales of the Revolution was repeated to the parents of the Little Washingtons; and Jim, too, had been warned never to speak of these stories, lest Mr. Vernon be forbidden to tell more of them. But the four children were not so wary between themselves; and, before John and his friends reached the Vernon Homestead, it had been agreed that, soon, the Little Washingtons would play that new game of raising horses and equipping men for the American forces. The added touch of rescuing a fugitive by hiding him in the furnace of the blacksmith shop made the plan the more alluring to try out at the first opportunity.

By this time they all had reached the farm-house, and to the joy of the Little Washingtons it was seen that the house, though smaller than Woodlawn, really was a miniature of the style of the mansion house at Mount Vernon. Indoors, too, were wonderful old pieces of furniture handed down in the Vernon family since the day of Grandpop Vernon, of Lexington fame.

In the kitchen was the old crane upon which hung the kettles and pots; and in every nook or corner one could see tiny cupboards. Low ceilings and small-paned windows showed the place to be many years old. Great four-poster beds, so high that it was necessary to climb up by means of tiny step-ladders, made the children laugh. And Martha said: "If you roll out of that bed, John, you'll feel it, all right."

Finally the inspection of the house and grounds ended and everybody pronounced themselves delighted with their resorts for the summer. Mr. Vernon was to take entire charge of the two farms, hiring such help as he needed and selling such produce as might not be used by the families. Fruit, vegetables, and milk, eggs, butter and meat would be paid for by the tenants exactly as if they had to purchase it at the markets. At the end of the season, Mr. Vernon's books would be balanced and the money would be equally divided between his tenants and himself. The farmer said this plan was too generous by far, since he expected nothing for the produce used by the two families. But he was silenced in his unselfish objections.

With such pleasant surroundings, and such a wonderful story-teller as this white-haired man would be, the Little Washingtons were looking forward to a grand time that summer. But before they continue their Washington Games, dear readers, you'd better know who they are and how they came to be in Vermont that summer.

In the first book, called *Little Washingtons,* the two Parke children, Martha and George Washington Parke, were introduced. Their two comrades, John Graham and the little colored boy Jim, also were introduced to you. How they lived near the City of Washington, on two adjoining estates, and how these four playmates enjoyed the fun of acting General Washington's life very closely, is told you.

In the next book, called *Little Washingtons' Relatives,* you learn about their cousins from Philadelphia, and how they had a real battle and siege with some bad boys that climbed over the back fence and hurled mud-balls at the children. These cousins were just as keen for playing Washington games, as the Parke children hoped they would be, and plenty of excitement and fun resulted from this visit.

In another book called *Little Washingtons' Travels* it tells how the children were taken with their parents on a trip to New York City; and, while staying in one of the large hotels with Granny (Jim's grandmother) to watch them while their parents went to a reception, the Little Washingtons strayed to the roof garden; there they staged such a battle as they never had had before or since. It lived in their memories ever after, and often was referred to as the Battle of New York Harbor.

In the fourth book called *Little Washingtons at School* the children are entered at a little country school a mile from their homes. But their delight in playing battle and sieges made lots of trouble for the teacher. Then one day the Little Washingtons discover a band of gypsies near the school; and, in capturing their stolen horses, the children unconsciously do a great good for the community.

Then in the fifth book called *Little Washingtons' Holidays,* you learn how, soon after school is closed for the summer, they spend their vacation days. Plans for going to a farm in Vermont

caused great anticipation. What they
played on the steamer on the way to
New York, brings you up to this story
of life on the farm.

CHAPTER II

HORSES FOR THE ARMY

BRIGHT and early on the morning following John's going to Vernon Homestead to live, George and Martha finished breakfast and, calling to Jim as they ran from the back door, started across the field by the footpath. The two Parke children had planned that morning that no time was to be lost before playing the Grandpop Vernon game. Since it was most evident that the present Mr. Vernon had a great fund of similar stories, that would make fine fun, there was no use in postponing the games until they got home again.

John was just as eager to put the story of the blacksmith into play, as his comrades were to do so. Therefore the little army of four started away to search for horses, or a substitute for them.

They had not been limited in the boundaries of how far they might go in their pursuit of pastime, because no one thought the children would leave the immediate vicinity of the houses. So they were not disobeying orders, when they sought here and there for their horses with which to supply the army.

At last, after an hour's vain search for animals, John stopped on top of a slight ascent of the land, and then smiled as he pointed to a herd of cows pasturing peacefully in a meadow beyond the woods.

"Did you ever ride a cow?" asked he, of his comrades.

"No, but they seem tame enough. No trouble riding them, I should say," replied George.

"Besides we could hold on to their horns, and that will help out fine in this case where we have no harness," said Martha.

"Yoh don' guess dem cows will buck, do yuh?" asked Jim.

"Mercy no! they're tame as tame can be," declared Martha.

So the four foragers for horses with which to supply the army started down the hill for the pasture. Several fences had to be climbed, and then at last they reached the lot where the cows solemnly chewed their cuds, or moved lazily around to seek a shady resting place.

George glanced back over his shoulder in the direction of the two houses. Not a sign of them could be seen, because the hill screened the meadow from view of all on the other side of it.

"Dey look moughty high up to me," commented Jim, dubiously.

"Yes; they do seem rather tall and broad, George," said Martha.

"Pooh! not nearly so high up as a horse would be," retorted George, bravely.

"You climb up on one first, and tell us how it feels," suggested John.

"The only trouble will be in *getting* up," remarked George, looking from the ground to the back of the nearest cow.

"You might climb up in that old apple tree and let yourself down upon the back of that black-and-white spotted cow under the tree, there," advised Martha, nodding in that direction.

"I think Jim could do that better than any of us," answered George, in a way meant to impress Jim with his value to his friends. This time, however, Jim failed to rise to the temptation.

"I don' know 'bout dat, George," returned the little pickaninny; "dem horns don' look quite inwitin' to me."

"Hoh!" retorted George, "a cow's horns are quite safe, Jim. She never uses them on people, you know."

"Whad foh she got dem den?" demanded Jim, instantly.

"Why," began Martha, not to urge Jim to ride the steed, but to show off her knowledge, "Nature never meant a cow to have horns; in fact, a cow is not one of Nature's manufactures, Jim. She is what they call a cross-bred animal, with a reindeer for a father and a tame milk-giving beast for a mother. That's how it happened."

"Mebbe yo'r right, Marfa," acknowl-edged Jim. "Kase I hearn my daddy talk of awful cross cows he had to milk one time. Mebbe dis one is one of dem crosses."

Nevertheless after a lengthy discus-sion on the subject of the gentleness of cows in general and this one in par-ticular, Jim was induced to try to ride the animal, which, to the Little Wash-ingtons, was a symbol of the horses raised and given to the Revolutionary army by Grandpop Vernon.

Jim was boosted up into the old apple tree and, when he had crawled out upon the down-sweeping bough pointed out to him, he found he could al-most touch the cow's back with his bare foot.

"Don't frighten her away, Jim," warned John, anxiously.

"Wait a second, Jim, till I get in front of her and call her 'Bossy,' in a nice soft tone," called Martha, in a low voice; at the same time she crept up be-side the cow and reached forth her hand to pat her neck, in order to distract her attention to that which might go on above her back.

George as usual chose the part where there would be the least danger and the most glory after the game was over with. He stood directly beneath the apple-tree bough and advised Jim.

"Mebbe John better git hol' on dem horns an' hol' fas' whiles Marfa abstracks th' cow's 'tention from me. Den I kin slie on widdout bein' yanked off. Onct I git my han's on her horns, den she kin go all she craves," suggested Jim, suspended just above the landing place where he hoped to sit.

John immediately sidled up to the cow on the opposite side from that where Martha stood engaging the cow's interest. The wondering bovine found no carrot or tidbit in the hand that reached out to her, and she could not understand why this should be. Then John tried to get a grasp on her horns, but he was too short—or the horns were too high.

Martha had just summoned up enough courage to step up before the cow's nose with a handful of grass extended in her hand. John, stretching himself by means of his toes, had reached up and caught a slight hold on the nearest horn. George, in his eagerness to urge Jim to let himself down without more loss of time, stood directly back of the cow and almost under the apple-tree bough.

Jim was leaning down watching John, planning to slide up on the broad, sleek back of the cow the moment he saw John get his grip on the only menace the beast had for the pickaninny. But the apple tree was weak from old age, and her arms could not hold up the least extra weight placed on it; so, with a faint crack of regret, the bough let go from the parent trunk.

Then came the tableau to Grandpop Vernon's work in the old Colonial Days! The cracking of the dry wood in the apple-tree bough, the unexpected switching of the branches upon the cow's back, and the hard thump of a boy's body striking her neck, made the cow act as she never acted before.

She lashed madly with her tail, whipping George across the face; her heels flew up and struck George in the stomach. Back he went flat upon the grass and remained there in a breathless condition for a time. The spring with which she let go her hind legs seemed to move her head and front legs also. She gave a sudden twist to her neck that, because he was clutching to her horn with might and main, lifted John momentarily from his feet. In such a neck-twirl, her face rammed Martha's face, and the cow sneezed and snorted at the contact, frightening the Little Washington lady almost stiff. Over she went, measuring her full length upon the sod, but screaming loudly and rolling frantically to keep out of the way of the beast. John's unlooked-for lifting from good old Mother Earth was not for long—he instantly let go his grip on the horn and fell down. But Jim! what of the brave little soldier who offered himself for a star part in this performance?

Well, Jim managed to hold to the

first object he found near his hands, and this proved to be the horns of the cow. Before he could yell for help and before his comrades could understand what was taking place Jim was being carried across the pasture-lot. Hanging on to those horns for dear life and being shaken and bumped all over the broad back of the cow, the pickaninny felt his eyes bulging from their sockets; and his double row of little white teeth almost chewed the end of his tongue off, every time he opened his mouth to scream. But Jim held fast to the only safety clutch he knew of!

Back and forth, and around the meadow galloped the cow, hoping to rid her back of the undesirable bumping. After several rounds, however, her breath gave out and she had to put on the slow brakes. Still Jim clung to the horns, though his thin arms felt like clay pipe-stems cracking to pieces.

It was a toss-up between the cow and Jim which would subside first. It proved to be the cow; for Jim's frenzied fear filled him with all the strength and perseverance which could trace its beginning 'way back to an African forefather.

The cow, at last, wobbled uncertainly as she came to a full stop on the brink of the pasture brook. Here she sank down, first kneeling upon her fore-legs as is the way with cows. This action lowered her head to the ground, and shot Jim clear over and dropped him down in the water. But the cow realizing quickly that the movable burden was gone from her neck, got up again and started across the meadow.

The brook was not deep, but the mud was. And Jim went head first into this mud. He managed to free his head and then get one hand out of the mud, then another, and finally he could stand up straight; his feet were embedded, however, and these he must pull loose before he could climb out of the water.

He got one bare foot free, but the other went deeper into the soft mud. When he struggled to free this one, he had to stand upon the one just lifted out. Thus pulling up one foot, then the other, without succeeding in the least in climbing out with *both* feet, Jim began to understand the work was not so simple as it might seem. He always had a faithful assistant with him, nevertheless, and that was his lung-power. He now gave that full play to call for help.

After rolling over on the grass to a place where she dared sit up and gaze about her, Martha saw what had happened. She had to dry her eyes upon her skirt, because the sneezing and snorting of the cow had sprinkled her face and blinded her eyes.

George was sprawled upon the ground, howling for help; and John was about to pick himself up from the place where the cow had dragged him. Martha was the first to catch sight of Jim riding the Army steed across the pasture lot.

"Oh, boys! Looka Jim go it!" cried she, jumping up and pointing excitedly at the runaway.

George forgot his howling and

scrambled to his feet, and John wheeled about to look in the direction Martha had indicated. All three Little Washingtons stood spell-bound and watched the race, and wondered as they watched how long Jim could hang on to the horns.

They were not kept in doubt very long. They saw the cow stop beside the brook and they saw what happened to Jim. Then they started across the pasture lot, but they took unusual pains to keep at a discreet distance from the cows. Finally they reached the bank of the stream.

"What're you doing with your feet, Jim?" called George, seeing his comrade marking time in the mud.

"I'se isn't doin' nuffin wid my feets, but dis mud is doin' it all," wailed Jim.

"Jim," tittered Martha, "you look just like the slaves did in olden times, when their cruel taskmasters made them tread out the grain or meal with their feet."

"Dis ain't no olden time, Marfa, ner

I ain't no slave. Anudder ting I ain't
—dat am a horse-trainer! No moh foh
me!"

At this dire statement from Jim, his
three comrades took alarm and tried
to pull him up out of the mud. What
would happen, should Jim refuse to
take part in future Little Washington
games? This must not be, so his
friends began at once to praise the manner in which he rode that cow, while
they had been disabled in the first assault.

CHAPTER III

NEW IDEAS FROM THE BOOK

FORTUNATELY for the future games of the Little Washingtons, both families were too busy with unpacking trunks and boxes to think of the children; hence the episode in the pasture-lot passed without others than the actors in it being the wiser.

Jim was washed with plenty of water, —seeing the brook was right at hand— then the four would-be trainers of army steeds trudged across the meadow and climbed the rail-fence back of the barns of Woodlawn.

"It feels as if it might be lunch time," hinted George.

Martha laughed. "That's because the cow helped your breakfast to digest so unexpectedly when she kicked you."

George gave his sister a brotherly scowl for her remark, and Martha giggled gleefully. John scoffed at such pleasantry and grumbled: "If one of you had been in the fix that Jim and I were in, you'd think of something besides such foolish talk."

"I wants to say right now," stated Jim, positively, "dat no one ain't goin' to make me do no jumpin' aroun' dis affernoon. I is sittin' still on a nice soft cushion somewhar."

"That's so! We forgot poor Jim must be awfully lame," exclaimed Martha, suddenly sobering as she remembered the rough-rider's bareback race across the meadow.

"We might get the Washington Farmer book, and read all afternoon," suggested George.

"That's what we will!" agreed his chums.

So this is how it came about that the Parkes and the Grahams discovered the four children safely seated upon porch cushions under a great old pine tree, taking turns in reading the story of General Washington's farm-life.

"I knew that book would have a quieting effect on their imagination," said Mrs. Parke, congratulating herself on her wisdom.

"The summer is not over yet," laughed Mr. Parke.

"Well, this is the second day of our vacation on the farm, and all's well thus far," returned Mrs. Graham.

What would these fond mothers have said had they witnessed the morning's attempt at providing army horses for Washington's Revolutionary soldiers?

"Suppose we read from the book wherever it happens to open first," suggested Martha, taking the volume and holding it up between her hands.

"That's a fine plan, and we won't complain if it opens at a dry place," agreed John.

"But I won't agree to have you go on reading more than one page of dry stuff," argued George.

"An' I don' wantta hear no moh 'bout ridin' Grandpop Veron's hosses," objected Jim, squirming on the cushion

as he remembered the morning's train-
ing-school for cows.

Martha proceeded to rest the book
upon her knees and let the covers open
of their own accord. Then she looked
curiously to see what chapter might be
their lot to read. "Oh, this is great!"
cried she; her attentive companions
looked expectant.

"It's a different explanation of a trip
Washington made to the wilds of Pennsylvania—we played the game once, but
it was not so good a description as this
one seems to be. Now listen:

"'In October Washington started
with his old friend Docter Craik and
three servants,—of which number Billy
Lee was one,—on the dangerous trip
to the western region of Pennsylvania.
The country was mostly unsettled, there
being only small hamlets few and far
between along the route.

"'By following the old Braddock
Road the travelers reached Pittsburgh,
which was a village of about a score
of cabins. At this place they secured
a dugout, and two Indians and several

Border men. These with Crawford and Washington's group formed the party which now voyaged down the Ohio, selecting rich bottom lands and at the same time enjoying fine sport hunting and fishing.

" 'This region was little known to white men. Daniel Boone had taken his first hunting trip into the "dark and bloody land of Kaintuckee" the year before, where the wigwams of Indians stood on the banks of the river.

" 'It was at one such Indian village that Washington met a chief who had been with him on his never-forgotten winter journey in 1753, when he went to warn the French.

" 'Between the Indians and the white men peace now seemed to reign, but rumors of uprisings were current, and the Red Man's ire would soon show itself again, once the spark made a fire.

" 'Washington's party heard a report that the Indians had killed two whites, but the story was unfounded; they learned later that a trader had tried to cross a ford of the Ohio on his horse and had been drowned.

" 'In spite of the uncertain temper of the Indians, the travelers continued to scout up the Great Kanawha River, near the mouth of which Washington located two vast tracts of land for himself and his comrades.

" 'After many interesting experiences in hunting and fishing the entire party turned back and finally reached home after an absence of nine weeks.' "

"Say, Martha," interrupted George, impatiently, "there isn't much fun to that page. Of course, we might take that boat on the pond and play we were Washington's party voyaging up the Ohio, but there isn't a single fight with the Indians, and not one story of how he got cornered by a bear or a wolf."

"If the book told us *something* about his fishing,—but it says only that he went fishing!" scorned John.

"I thought it would have been more exciting, from the way it started out," admitted Martha. "But I can see myself how dry it sounds."

"Let me have the book and see where it opens," demanded George, thinking possibly that the volume would open at a more exciting section of the farm-story if he held the covers. Martha gave him the book without demur, and George held it as he had watched his sister hold it.

It opened at the same place, but George refused to confess it. He permitted his glance to pass over the familiar lines of text and rest upon a paragraph at the foot of the second page. Here he began to read the following:

"'December 23, 1783, Washington resigned his commission as Chief of the American Army and started for Mount Vernon to keep Christmas at home for the first time since 1774.

"'He was kept engaged in building up and improving his home estate for many months thereafter; then in September, 1785, he set off on horseback to visit his western lands again and to inquire into a scheme he had planned for navigation on the Potomac, which might lead up to a connection with the head waters of the Ohio.

" 'With him went old Doctor Craik, as of yore, and their suite consisting of several servants and six horses; also the outfit of food, utensils, medicines, and hunting or fishing necessities, wine and clothing.

" 'On the way they stopped at taverns for meals, when such an opportunity was possible; and they sojourned at the homes of acquaintances at night, at times when they could arrive in time to do so. At other times they camped and roughed it.' "

"George, that page is just as dry as the one Martha read," complained John, grumblingly. "I'd rather go to the barn and ride the donkey, than sit here listening to that stuff."

"Well, then, you take the book and see where it opens," suggested George, anxious to please John, but not willing to get up and start for the barn. His ribs still ached from the prodding the cow had given him in the forenoon.

John gladly took the book and allowed it to open at will. "Oh, see where I got it!" exclaimed he, displaying a page in the back part of the volume, which spoke of Washington's trips.

" 'Washington took a mild interest in fishing, but most of it was done with a seine. Occasionally he would take a boat-trip down the Potomac and, with hook and line, fish for sport. He and Doctor Craik had fishing tackle with them on both their western journeys and they certainly made use of it in the mountain streams, as well as in the Ohio River.

" 'At the Federal Convention in 1787 Washington went with Gouverneur Morris to Valley Forge, presumably to revisit the old camp but really to fish for trout. They lodged at the house of a widow, and during the stay had rather good luck with the fishing.' "

"Just wait a moment, John, 'til I make a note of that," asked George, taking a stubby bit of a pencil from his pocket and looking about for a scrap of paper upon which to write.

"Use the margin of that old newspaper at your feet," suggested Martha, nodding to a scrap of yellowed paper on the grass.

"I just want to say that that trout fishing trip will make a good game— what page is that on, John?" explained George, as he tore off the strip of paper and waited to make a memo of the page in the book. Then John was told to proceed with the story.

"I'll skip a few paragraphs which are of no account," ventured John, turning the pages, "and begin here, where there's a story about his fishing.

" 'Farmer Washington was fond of fish as an article of diet and he wanted them fresh for his table. An old black slave at Mount Vernon, reported to be the son of an African King, tried to keep the household supplied with fresh fish. It was his duty to go out on the river in a skiff and catch the perch, bass, and rockfish.

" 'It is told how old Jack would often fall asleep while sitting in the boat waiting for a bite; then the impatient cook, whose duty it was to serve the meals promptly at the hour, would send messengers to find the tardy fisherman.

"'Jack hearing the repeated roaring from those shouting at him from the shore would pull up his lines and start back home. His mess of fish generally acted as his judge: when small, he was condemned for being a "lazy, shif'less niggeh!" when abundant, he was commended for being "de bestes' fishaman on de Ribeh."'"

"I'll just take down another note there, John; all these short stories will make one good long game, I think," remarked George; and his friends agreed heartily that they would.

"Here's a page which tells of Washington's hunting trips. I can't find another word about his fishing," said John, after turning several pages for added information on fishing.

"I don't think we ought to mix the hunting game with the fishing, George," said Martha. "If we play Washington going a-fishing, we will have to sail out on the pond, or stand on the banks; and that will not work in very well with hunting, or riding to hounds,—now will it?"

"Martha's right, John. We'd better leave the reading of the hunting days wait for another time," advised George.

In turning the pages of the book in a haphazard manner, waiting for his friends to suggest something for him to read, John caught sight of this interesting paragraph and read it aloud:

" 'Benjamin Franklin knew the great men of his time on earth, and near the close of his life he wrote in his will: "My fine crabtree walking-stick with the gold head, curiously wrought to form the cap of Liberty, I bequeath to my good friend, and the friend of every one, George Washington. If it could be transformed from a mere stick into a mighty sceptre, I know he would wield it with justice and wisdom." ' "

Martha nodded her head approvingly: "That's a fine line. Can't you find a few more like that one?"

George was about to object to the reading of maxims and "fine lines," but

John anticipated the interruption, and said, " 'Here are two copies of writing that Washington had to do in his daily lessons in penmanship. They sound just like our General—listen: 'Get what you get honestly; use what you get frugally; that's the way to live comfortably and die honorably.'

"And this is another one: 'Humility is the forerunner of advancement and honor; ambition is the harbinger of destruction and ruin.' "

As John concluded the second maxim George jumped up and spoke hastily: "That's enough for to-day, John. We've got to go down to the pond now, and look over the place for the game of fishing. Better leave the book on the verandah table, so it won't get dirty."

So John ran over to the verandah and placed the volume upon the wicker table; then he hurried after his comrades, who were on their way to the pond.

They walked around the small sheet of water for a short distance, then Martha mentioned the boat.

"Maybe it isn't fastened with a pad-lock," hinted she.

"Let's go and see," quickly returned George. And in a moment the four Little Washingtons were running back along the footpath to inspect the anchorage of the flat-bottomed rowboat.

"Goody!" cried George, under his breath, in order to avoid attention from elder persons that might command them to keep out of the fishing smack—for that is what it meant to the four friends.

"We can play this is the mouth of the Potomac, and the stream which leads from the pond away into the woods can be the River that ran past Mount Vernon," suggested Martha.

"It's too late to play that game this afternoon, but we can go and dig the bait and try to find fishing tackle for the four of us to use to-morrow," advised George.

"I kin tell yuh whar a hull lot of fish-worms kin be dug dis minit!" declared Jim, finding his opportunity to say a word.

"Where? where? where?" echoed his three confederates eagerly.

"In th' chicken-yard. I see'd Mr. Wernon a-diggin' up dat groun' dis mawnin' and sech a lot of squirmy worms yuh neber see'd in yor life! He tole me dey was good fer hens; da's why he liked to turn ober th' groun' fer 'em."

"Let's hurry there and see if we can dig any and keep them in an old can for the morning," said John, starting away.

"We can borrow Mr. Vernon's spade from the tool-house," called George, as they ran along.

"Jim might ask his mammy for a tomato can—if she has one in the kitchen," suggested Martha, as they all neared the chicken-yard.

John got the shovel and a spade, and Jim came back with an empty tomato-can, and then the digging began. George and John dug, while the other two were supposed to pick up the worms and drop them into the can.

When Martha saw the squirming, wriggling strings of worms, however, she shuddered and refused to pull them from the dirt.

"How yoh goin' to push 'em on a hook, ef yuh feels dat way now?" demanded Jim, handing her the can, and stooping to grab the worms before they could get back in the ground.

The children found an abundant crop of fish-worms there, and the can was more than half filled before Martha said, "We can't use all these in one day! Better leave a few worms in the earth for Mr. Vernon's chickens."

"I suppose we can always come back and dig for more, if we run short any time," said George, stretching his lame back-muscles.

"Then we'll put away the spades and go hunt for tackle," was John's answer, as he started from the coop.

CHAPTER IV

WASHINGTON'S FISHING GAME

AS soon as John could get away from the house the following morning he scampered across the field, shouting to his comrades as he ran. Jim had been posted out under the big pine tree near the turn-stile which led to the field-path; therefore, the moment he saw John coming he hurried to the side verandah and signaled for George and Martha, by sounding the tin whistle that he had brought from Virginia.

In a short time thereafter the four Little Washingtons were to be seen running away from the house and following the path which led to the barnyard. This George advised, because it might not be well for their excursion should the elders see them taking the footpath to the pond—and the row-boat.

Fortunately for the fishermen John had discovered two bamboo fishpoles with hooks and lines in the shed at his house. George and Martha had begged some twine and long pins from Granny, without explaining what purpose the pins would be used for.

Jim said he knew how to use bent pins in fishing, and they all knew how to cut poles from the young trees to provide extra fishpoles for themselves.

"I thought we might have to fish longer than the morning," said Martha, with a knowing wink, "so I brought some cookies and a few cold boiled eggs for a luncheon."

"Oh, gee! That's fine, Marth!" exclaimed George.

"We never thought of that; but we could play we were on a Pittsburgh and Ohio camping trip, couldn't we?" said John, eagerly.

"Do you s'pose they caught perch and bass in the Ohio?" asked George, dubiously. "The book mentioned those

fish as being in the Potomac; and we all
know that the Potomac would be half
salt and half fresh water, because the
Cheseapeake Bay backs up at high tide,
you see."

Martha chuckled as she replied:
"We're going to catch any kind of fish
that pond provides. They may be
perch, or they may be the canaries that
swing on the perch!"

The children thought this such a
fine pun that they all laughed hilari-
ously, until John suddenly hushed them.
"We'll be found out, if we make so
much noise. Then what of our game?"

That was quite enough to silence the
slightest giggle thereafter, and they
trudged on quietly, whispering if it became necessary to communicate with
each other.

The boat had not been padlocked to
the tree, and it was a simple matter to
undo the old rope. There were no oars
to be seen, and, it being unwise to ask
for any at the house, the fishermen used
two long sticks which were found under
the trees near the pond. They planned

to use these to pole themselves around the pond.

"Now Jim must sit up in the prow, and Martha can sit on the seat at the stern," suggested George, taking command as usual. "John and I will do the poling, then when you think we have come to a good fishing-ground, we will anchor and all begin to fish."

"What will you anchor with, seeing you have no anchor?" tittered Martha, teasing her brother as was her custom when he tried to show off before the rest of them.

George looked at John, then he asked: "Do you s'pose we could roll one of those big stones into the boat for an anchor? It will be an easy matter to tie this end of rope around the rock, if we once get it inside the boat."

"Sure!" agreed John, eagerly. "And when we lift the rock to roll it overboard to anchor us, we might sing the sailor's ditty; you know—the one about 'heaving her over, me lads.' It will make us feel that we are 'sailing the main' and 'breasting the gales.'"

"Come on, then," ordered George, springing from the boat, and followed by John. Martha and Jim sat waiting while the two boys tried to move the stone George had selected for an anchor.

"Good gracious! It doesn't *look* so heavy," grunted John, seeing the rock would not budge from its resting place on the earth.

"We'll have to be satisfied with a smaller one," replied George, grudgingly. So the two boys sought another rock, and finding one nearer the boat availed themselves of that for the anchor.

By dint of shoving and rolling, and short distances of carrying it, the two boys finally got it over to the side of the boat.

"Now, John, when I am ready and call out 'Heave-ho!' you must bend your back to the burden." George felt that he had spoken in a fine nautical fashion, but his hearers paid scant heed to him: they were too engaged in watching the anchor come over on board.

Both boys spat upon their hands and then prepared to lift the rock up. At the same time John tried to concentrate on the word for hoisting.

"Now, ready! Then grip a hold underneath it," said George.

Both boys stooped and placed their hands securely under the rock. Martha and Jim suspended their breathing, if by this means it would help swing the anchor aboard.

"Now, my hearty—heave, ho!" shouted George, at the same time doing his part by lifting mightily.

John lifted, too, but his one hand slipped from its hold. The rock had been hoisted about a foot from the ground, and the slipping of John's hand on the side nearest the water caused the weight to over-balance. Before either John or George could stop it, the rock anchor had toppled over and rolled into the water with a splash! A shower of water sprinkled the two in the boat, and that was the last of that anchor.

George scowled and would have blamed the mishap on John, had not the crackling of twigs on the other side of the strip of woods warned the children to forego an anchor and get away from shore. It might be Mr. Vernon, or it might be one of their daddies! Then this Washington fishing game would come to naught.

"We really can do without an anchor, anyway," remarked George, once they were poling safely away from the shore.

"Sure!" agreed John; "the water is not deep, and we can ram one of the poles down into the mud to anchor by."

The flat-bottomed boat was very solidly built, and the weight of it in shallow water made it hard to shove with no other power to move it than the small arms of the children and the slender sticks of wood they used. Nevertheless the four Little Washingtons continued pushing and breathing hard, thinking they were having a very exciting game.

"If one or two of us got out the boat might go faster," suggested George, looking at Martha and Jim for the expected victims for the sacrifice.

"Jim doesn't weigh more'n a feather, and I'm sure *I* am not going to give up my fun!" declared Martha, with a toss of the head.

John generally sided with Martha, even though she was a girl, because she had more spirit and frankness in her attitude to her playmates. Now he said: "If we separated the group we started in the wilderness with it will spoil all the fun."

"But we can play Jim is the old African that goes fishing every day in the Potomac," argued George.

"And what would you have me be?" demanded Martha.

"W-h-hy—you could be the cook that gets so mad waiting for Jack to bring the fish home."

"Then where will you and John be, while we are at Mount Vernon?" asked Martha, suspiciously.

"John and I will be Washington and Crawford, or Dr. Craik on that Pittsburgh journey."

"Well," decided Martha, emphatically, "you be the cook at the farm, and *I* will be Washington this time."

This undreamed-of plan was so impossible for George to think of that he quickly changed his mind about having extra weight in the boat. He said nothing, but he went to work with zeal to try to push the craft faster than before.

"Maybe it will go better if both you boys push on the same side," suggested Martha, after a lapse of time.

"Then we might take the wrong course," objected George. "Don't we want to sail down to the stream that flows from this pond?"

"Yes; but you can shove good and hard on one side, then shove on the other—both shoving at the same time," explained Martha. "Shall I show you what I mean?"

But George never liked to be shown. He thought he knew it all, and he refused Martha's offer to demonstrate her meaning.

"You move up a step, John, and let

me stand beside you on that side. We'll try out Martha's idea, even if it doesn't work."

So John moved along, and George came over to his side of the boat. Both boys drove their poles down on the same side and at the same time. The boat responded beautifully and shot ahead at least three feet. The four Washingtons grinned with relief at this.

"This time we'll send her six feet!" bragged John.

"Push your pole away down deep and then shove," suggested Martha. "George doesn't ram the pole down straight enough—he lets it go on too much of a slant to give him any driving power."

"Do you mean I should do it like this?" asked her brother, at the same time jamming the pole down almost straight from where he stood leaning over the side of the boat.

John saw him drive, and he obeyed orders to drive at the same time, so he sent the pole down and then bent back to provide the leverage. George's pole went down straight, all right, but it went deep down in the soft mud and, when he leaned on the upper half to shove, the old wood snapped in the middle. Over went George into the water!

The unexpected exit of one of the polers sent the boat in a circular sweep half-round its length, so that the remaining sailors in the craft found George aft instead of beside the boat. He was spluttering and trying to summon help. The pond was so shallow that there was no danger of drowning, but the mud was soft and clung to the boy's shoes.

After much straining and pulling and puffing for breath, the four were re-assembled in the boat again, George dripping wet, with legs and feet caked with the black mud; and his comrades drying the perspiration from their faces and necks after such exertion.

"Phew!" ejaculated Martha, with face red as a peony. "We ought to have a Carnegie Medal for life-saving after that."

"You ought to have a dose of that

mud yourself," snarled George, morosely. "It was your fault that I had to change sides and help John pole the way you advised me to."

John realized what the end of this fine game would be if the sister and brother continued an argument such as this promised to be, hence he quickly threw "oil on the troubled waters"— though the water in the pond needed no oil; it was so stirred from its muddy bottom that it would take time to clarify again.

"We're almost down near the place where the pond runs into the river," was his encouraging call.

All heads turned to verify this statement and Martha said, "I'll take George's place and pole for a time."

George sat in his sister's place and watched for a chance to find fault with her work, but she knew he wanted to do this, so she was extra careful not to give him the chance.

Finally the boat moved into the stream which wound its way through the woods, and here the children found both banks hidden from sight by the tall reeds growing along the edge of the water.

"My daddy tol' me dat down in Alabam' dey cotches mos' bes' fish in reedy water," said Jim, studying his pole and tackle eagerly.

"Maybe we ought to pole over to one of those sides and try Jim's suggestion," ventured Martha, looking at George.

"All right, go over and we'll try," conceded he.

So the boat was moved over where the reeds grew thickest, and John offered to anchor it for a time by means of digging the pole down in the mud and holding to the upper part of it.

"Jim, you've got your hook all baited and ready—you drop your line over first," advised Martha, trying to unsnarl her hook from John's line, where it had caught during so much changing of places when the children poled from the sides of the boat.

Eager to catch the first fish for the great General's dinner, Jim flung his hook out amongst the reeds. Fortunately it did not catch on the marsh-weeds, but fell between two small bogs where a large flat stone separated them.

George selected the stern of the boat from which to fish, believing he would have better luck by angling just beyond the edge of the reedy growth. John had to steady the boat by leaning heavily upon the sunken pole; and Martha was still fumbling with the hooks.

Suddenly John cried excitedly, "See there! Jim's got a bite!" All heads leaned over to see the tiny ripple on the water just in front of the big stone.

"S-s-sh!" warned George, holding up his hand for quiet. "If you make a noise, the fish will hurry away. We must keep silent."

But the fish had no idea of hurrying away. It seemed to like the taste of Jim's angle worm, and the biting became more pronounced. Jim trembled with suppressed excitement—to think he was going to catch the first fish!

Then the cork went under water suddenly, but as quickly bobbed up again.

The children gasped with the thrill of the fisherman. Eyes almost popped with the strain of watching that cork!

A few seconds of peace at the end of the fishline, and then Jim felt it begin to jiggle again. Also the tiny ripples began to circle once more upon the placid water. The biting at the bait got stronger, and then, to the joy of four Little Washingtons, the cork began to be dragged quickly through the water.

"Catch him! Catch him!" yelled George, forgetting his recent advice to keep silence or the fish would run away.

"Pull him in, Jim!" shouted John, forgetting the anchor pole and waving both hands and arms to show Jim how to yank in the fish.

"Don't let him get away with the hook and bait, Jim!" cried Martha, anxiously.

Between so many cross-fires Jim acted automatically and gave a hard pull on the line. It resisted. All eyes gazed in awed surprise.

"Gee! that's a whopper!" exclaimed

George, edging over to Jim's side. "Hold fast, and we'll help you haul him in."

The "we" in the offer to help was guarantee for John and Martha to assist. So all four fishermen now began to advise and try to land their wonderful fish. Jim had been unconsciously left to the lesser joy of holding the pole, while George and John handled the taut line, bringing it in hand over hand.

Martha knelt upon the bottom of the boat, her face almost touching the water, as she tried to peer down to see the fish. "I see an *awful* big one, fighting against you boys!" screamed she, shrilly, pointing at something which really looked like a large, fat fish.

"Don't play him any longer," gasped George, breathless with excitement; "let *me* give him a clear swing and land him over the side of the boat. If he strikes the edge he will free himself and escape!"

Jim feared this would happen, and he managed to push his head between the two boys at the side of the boat; from this place he could see, even if he was not helping in the haul.

In another moment the Little Washingtons had the shock of a fisherman's luck—at the end of Jim's line came a queer looking thing for a perch or a bass or a trout,—such as they thought a Washington should catch. It fell with a thud upon the floor of the boat, and its funny feet clawed hold of the slats across the bottom; then it quickly freed itself from the hook and line.

My! how it could move over that flooring! The children watched spellbound as the mud-turtle ran hither and thither, seeking an exit for itself. Finally four little fishermen found their voices.

"A snapping-turtle!" yelled George, scrambling upon the seat at the stern of the boat just as the turtle ran where he had crouched a moment before.

"Get out of the way—quick!" cried John, seeing the turtle turn and make for him.

In backing unexpectedly into Martha without knowing the direction he was taking John caused Martha to lose her balance as she still knelt half-over the rim of the boat. In another second her other half was over, too, and a great shower of water sprayed the three remaining in the boat.

The moment Jim had heard the name "snapping-turtle" he had managed to get up out of harm's way, by balancing himself upon the very end of the prow, clinging there by means of both thin little hands. When Martha went overboard so suddenly, the boat rocked with the dragging on one side, then the release of the weight which had pushed it down. This rocking was too much for Jim, and he rolled off into the bottom of the boat just as the mud-turtle scampered in that direrction.

Then there was pandemonium let loose! Jim clawing and kicking and yelling, and John and George shouting advices, first to Jim, then to Martha, who thrashed about in the reeds in fear of forcing an acquaintance with the turtle's family. And to cap the climax of this fishing party the boat overturned, releasing the captured turtle and frightening four Little Washingtons out of a year's growth!

Their shrill cries and shouts echoed across the pond and reached Mr. Vernon. He was standing at the time telling Pete how glad he was to have children about the place again; then both men turned to listen. They rushed away, expecting to see a fatal ending to some awful accident to the children.

What they did find, however, made both Pete and the farmer laugh so heartily that the Little Washingtons felt annoyed. The four had managed to drag themselves from the muddy edge of the stream up to the sloping bank where they stood allowing the water and mud to trickle away from them back to its native element again.

"Why, Jim!" exclaimed Pete, trying to control his mirth, "what makes you seem so frightened? The water isn't deep."

"I foun' dat out back in the pon' whar George was dumped, but I diden' know dey kep' snappin' turkles in Wermont waters. Yoh tol' me dey growed down Souf."

Then the story of how the mud-turtle was caught made the two men laugh again, to the intense disapproval of the fishermen. Without so much as a scornful glance at the laughing elders George led his comrades away from the water where they had such disastrous results in fishing, and went on to the barns, where they hoped to clean the mud from their clothing before appearing before their families.

CHAPTER V

READING NEW GAMES

THE morning after the fishing excursion the four little friends met under the old pine tree near the field-path, and the Washington book was placed upon John's knee to be opened and read.

"We'll do just as we did the last time," advised George, "let it open where it will, and read from the first page whatever is there."

"If it proves to be too dry for us to play a game with, we'll stop you and look for another place," added Martha. Jim never had a word to say in these matters, because he could not read, so he took no part in the business part of it.

John found the book had opened at a chapter on sheep. "This promises to be fine!" declared he, hastily. "We said something about the fun it would be to shear our sheep—remember?" and John sent a significant glance at Jim's kinky wool.

Martha and George giggled understandingly, and urged John to begin the reading.

" 'Sheep raising was not profitable then because of dogs and wolves attacking them. Washington had various breeds but none with much merit as far as fleece or health was concerned. He kept the Holland or rat-tailed breed, several Spanish sheep, and a West Indian variety which looked more like goats with a scanty growth of wool.

" 'In those days when the rich masters kept so many hunting dogs, and the slaves had from an average of two to ten curs to a family, it is little wonder that so many sheep were killed by dogs. Wolves were such a menace that rewards were offered everywhere for their capture dead or alive. Generally the victor who brought in his wolf for the reward brought a dead beast! There is one account of how a countryman brought in two wolf whelps which he had found in a den when the she-wolf was off on a foraging quest. As the Squire was about to order the reward paid over to the man, a great commotion began at the door to the office.

" 'The Squire rapped for order, then bawled for silence, but the next minute revealed that which put an end to all ideas of peace and order in the place: the mother-wolf had tracked the man who had stolen her young and was now leaping down the aisle—an aisle which was quickly widened for her approach.

" 'The man seated upon the raised platform trying to mete out justice took to his heels without ceremony and was seen flying through the door behind his chair. Dignity was thrown to the winds, when a she-wolf came upon the scene.

" 'Several men at the door, having hurried to take up their guns, fired a volley just as the furious animal reached the pair of cubs at the foot of the judgment seat.' "

"Ah!" was the sympathetic sigh coming from Martha at this story. "Doesn't it seem a shame that the poor mother was shot?"

The boys took a more practical view of the case, however.

"If that wolf had caught your baby and was about to devour it, you'd want it shot right off," declared George.

"And that's what wolves do, Martha," added John. "They catch the little babies of all the other beasts of the forests; and kill folks, too! We must exterminate them, whenever we find them."

"Yeh," agreed Jim, catching at the word John had just used. "My daddy sayed he saw a man onct, what caught extermanitis from a mad animal. Dey had to take a red-hot poker and burn out all th' pizen from dat bite."

Since the children could not interpret the word Jim had just used so fluently, and none of them would show his or her ignorance by asking Jim what it meant, the subject was quickly changed.

"I'll continue the reading now," announced John. " 'The hogs on Washington's farms received little care, but were allowed to run half-wild in the woods. They were fed for a short period before being slaughtered, in order to produce a decent rasher of bacon when brought to the house to be used.

" 'Now and then Washington's horses met with accidents. The aged ones, too decrepit for use, were generally sold or disposed of; not because their owner was hard-hearted, but the necessity of keeping down the labor and time to care for them was the cause.

" 'One horse named Jolly had a right-foreleg crushed, and this was mended as best the men knew how. Washington investigated the matter and had Jolly swung up in a canvas hammock to keep the animal from moving the leg. Several days later, however, Jolly fell out of the swing and injured himself so badly that he had to be shot.' "

"John, was that little bit on sheep the only story for us to follow?" asked George, at this point of the reading.

"I'll turn back and see," said John, turning back a few pages. "Just before that part we read there is more about sheep; but I think we heard that before, the day Martha read to us on the train. Remember: where it says Washington had such poor sheep in the beginning, but improved the stock so that in 1789 he sheared an average of five pounds of wool from each one?"

The audience remembered, so John was not expected to repeat anything already noted for a future game. Instead he was asked to find a story which might adapt itself to a nice game for that day.

"The sheep game and the shearing will have to wait for a time when we can have plenty of time to fix up a water-trough and also borrow mother's scissors, you know," said Martha.

"What do you know about a water-trough?" asked George.

"I asked Mr. Vernon how sheep were sheared, and he told me they had to be scrubbed and washed first, as they passed through a sort of trough from one basin to the next, in order to thoroughly get the dirt and vermin from their fleeces. Then they were ready for shearing," explained Martha.

"He ain't got no sheep on dis fahm," announced Jim.

"How do you know?" demanded three anxious voices.

"Kase my daddy sayed to mammy dis mawnin' how she'd oughter keep her hair better oiled down er someun mought mistook her fer a black sheep an' try to shear her wool. Den dey bofe laffed an' I sayed to my daddy how we wuz goin' to use th' fahm sheep fer sech shearin'. Den dey laffed louder, an' my mammy sayed Mistah Wernon didn't keep no sheep on dis fahm—dey was all goats what had to take the lef' side at judgment day."

"Oh, your daddy and mammy were only joking, Jim. If we wander around this farm, I bet we'll find a great flock of sheep on some hillside," was Martha's encouraging explanation.

John had turned over several pages during this talk, and now he seemed to brighten up. "Listen to this and tell me

what you think of it for a good game."
Then he read:

" 'Washington was one of the first
farmers in America to attempt the raising of mules. He had heard of the
jackasses of Spain, but he learned that
the law forbade the exporting of them.
Through the friendship of the Spanish
minister of state, however, the General
was presented with two jacks and two
jennets.

" 'One of the jacks died on the trip
across the sea, but the three survivors
reached Mount Vernon in due season.
The jack was christened "Royal Gift,"
since he was sent to Washington by per-
mission of the king. He was an enormous beast, fifteen hands high, and his
body in proportion to his height. His
ears measured fourteen inches in length,
and his legs were long and muscular.
His lung-power was tremendous, and it
was spoken of by the General in a
humorous manner.

" 'At a later time Lafayette sent
Washington the gift of another jack
and two jennets from the Island of

Malta. These animals landed in good condition, though they were smaller beasts than those from Spain.

" 'Then Farmer Washington began breeding a cross-strain of jacks and horses which gave him the many mules that he worked on his estates thereafter. He praised these mules to a friend, calling them "excellent animals, cheap to upkeep and willing to work." But he said nothing of their tendency to balk.' "

Martha interrupted the reading here. "We could have lots of fun playing a balky mule game, boys."

"I was just thinking that we could try the old donkey in the stable and play he was one of Washington's mules," added George.

"He ain't no donkey," declared Jim, glad to show his wisdom. "He am a reel live jack sech as Washerton got f'om Spain. Ef yuh don' b'lieve it, measure his ears."

"Then he will make the fun all the better!" exclaimed Martha. "Where does Mr. Vernon take him so early every morning, and bring him back after sundown?"

"Dat we mus' fin' out. Kase it's suah dat we cain't use no jack what ain't goin' to be foun' at han' to use," was Jim's true suggestion.

"Make a note of those facts, George," advised Martha, and then she told John to proceed with the reading.

"Here's a story how Washington went fox-hunting. We haven't heard any of his hunting trips yet—only about his fishing."

"His fishing games are no good!" condemned George, instantly, and his three friends heartily agreed with him.

"Then we might try hunting, next time," said John, getting ready to read. 'On the days when Washington went hunting he would eat breakfast by candlelight. This meal usually consisted of corn cakes and milk. Then just before daybreak he, with his friends all well-mounted, would follow Billy Lee who was Master of Hounds at these excursions, to start up a fox.

" 'None rode so fearlessly or cheered

more loudly than did the General at a successful issue to the hunt.

"'It was usually a gray fox which was found in that section of the country; later, however, the red fox could be seen occasionally. At one of these hunting parties the riders—or the dogs, to be exact—started up a fine black fox. The animal led them a chase of over twenty miles through rough country, then disappeared again in the place where it had been found. This sable fox led the hunters many a chase, and sorry looking men they were at the end of these runs; yet the fox always managed to elude men and dogs.

"'Now and then Mrs. Washington and her lady-guests would ride out to watch the hunts, but they chose better roads than those the hunters took cross country. The ladies would try to be in at the death, however, and the brush would fall to the lot of the honored lady guest at the time.' There are plenty of short stories here about Washington's fox-hunting. They seem to be entries in a diary, giving dates and

places, but very little story to either,
that will make a good game for us,"
remarked John, glancing down the
page.

"That one about going on the fox-
hunt early in the morning is all right,"
said George. "We can play the whole
game."

"Yes," agreed Martha, eagerly. "We
might begin just as Washington did—
by getting up before dawn some morning, and fixing an early breakfast in
the kitchen. Maybe we can try some
corn cakes with syrup. I'd rather have
syrup than milk."

"So would we," confessed John.

"Say! I saw'd a man leave a jug ob
'lasses dis wery day!" exclaimed Jim,
gladly. "He tol' my mammy dat it war
genuwine Wermont maple surp. I
tastesed it next time I wuz alone in th'
pantry an' it shuah done tastes like fine
'lasses, all right!"

"You keep an eye on that jug, Jim,
'cause we will want it the morning we
go hunting," ordered George. The
children felt that what belonged to their

family, belonged likewise to them; no one had ever deprived them of feeling absolutely free to go and come at any time or in any place of their homes, so now they thought nothing of advising Jim to watch Washington's commissary department for them.

"After our breakfast, what?" asked John.

"Then we go out to the stables, mount our horses and call to Billy Lee (that's Jim, of course) to start off with the dogs," explained George.

"But we haven't any dogs," complained Martha.

"Nor horses for hunting," added John.

"Well, we just have to find some, that's all!" declared George. "Where there's a will, there's a way."

"Mr. Vernon said something to Pete last night about a few old horses he pastured across the field for people that wouldn't kill these old friends, yet they could not use them any more account of their old age," hinted Martha, meaningly.

"And I saw a nice old Newfoundland dog at the barns over at Vernon Homestead," added John.

"One dawg is 'bout all I kin manage at onct," said Jim, a smile lighting his face.

"Then that's settled!" was George's undisputed decision. "We breakfast at daybreak, haste to our steeds which will be at the pasture we heard of to-day, then follow Jim with his Vulcan, to seek and kill the black fox! Isn't that a great game?"

And the delighted Little Washingtons agreed that it promised to be a wonderful game!

CHAPTER VI

LITTLE WASHINGTONS' FOX-HUNTING

ACCORDING to the strict advices from Martha to act quickly, but quietly, they were creeping around at daybreak preparing for the great game of fox-hunting as described in Washington's storybook.

John had the farthest to come, but he also had the old shaggy Newfoundland dog to lead by a rope; hence he was rather late for a breakfast of corn cakes and maple 'lasses. Before he got indoors, however, he saw the smoke curling from the kitchen windows and he could smell burning flour.

"Hurry in, John," whispered George, in a scarcely understood voice, seeing he had his mouth filled with bread upon which the maple syrup had been poured until no more would remain on it.

"You get your plate, John, while I serve these corn cakes,—just like Washington used to have," bragged Martha, who was cook for the hunters just then.

John brought his plate obediently, but he looked askance at the blackened, soggy objects which had been given the name of corn cakes. Martha placed one upon his plate, then was about to take up another one, when John delayed her.

"Don't bother with another one for me, Martha; 'cause I'm not so very hungry this morning."

"Oh, but you have to eat them, John!" declared Martha. "I mixed a whole bowl full of batter, and we have to eat it."

John then saw with horror that a huge yellow bowl was full, just as Martha said, with some heavy mixture never known before to be called corn-cake-batter. At least, it was very different from the batter John had seen his cook stir and bake.

"George says he will eat his share, when he finishes his bread and syrup.

And Jim is eating all he can—see?" said Martha.

Poor little Jim was chawing away on the heavy soggy cakes, trying to please Martha; but he dared not express an opinion on her art of cooking. John had received two more cakes upon his plate while he stood arguing, and now he hurried from Martha's vicinity at the stove, and went over to George's side.

"You going to swallow these brick-bats?" asked he of George.

"I should say not!" returned George, watching his sister with guarded eyes, to see that she was not listening.

"Then I won't, either!" declared John, pushing his plate away. "I'll eat plain bread and syrup like you are."

"You have to *pretend* you ate them," warned George. "You can pick them up one by one and throw them back of the flour barrel in that corner behind us."

Jim overheard this advice and instantly took advantage of the "safety first" method of ridding himself of the need of eating the cakes. Thinking her guests had enjoyed their cakes, because they disappeared so rapidly, Martha came over with a fresh supply. These were not burnt so black, but they were half-cooked, and the batter dripped out here and there.

"Martha, we boys have finished our breakfast, and you haven't started yours," said George, anxiously. "When we are ready to go, we start whether you are eating or not."

John grinned expectantly, hoping to see Martha try to eat her own cakes, but she disappointed them this time.

"Oh, I finished my breakfast before you boys came in. I'm only serving you 'til you're through, then I shall start out."

"Goodness sakes! We're through *now!*" retorted John, not able to toss the cakes away while the cook was beside his chair.

"We might give those cakes to Bruno," suddenly thought John aloud. "The poor dog hasn't had breakfast yet."

Without waiting to hear what Martha might say to his proposal John caught up the plate and ran from the room. A moment later they heard him coaxing the Newfoundland to eat the cakes.

How long they may have dallied over breakfast cannot be told; but a suspicious moving around in the room overhead warned them to be off, or the fox hunting would come to naught that day.

Perhaps Bruno was as thankful to be spared eating those doughy cakes as John had been; because he trotted at their heels in a surprisingly lively manner, the moment they turned to run down the lane which led to the woodland pasture, where they had learned the horses were pastured.

It was a long walk for little legs, and before the Washingtons reached the pasture, they wished they had another breakfast, but a *real* one this time!

"We never remembered the guns!" exclaimed John, suddenly, when they came in sight of the old horses in the lot.

"Gee! we could have taken some weapons from that old box in the attic, had we thought of it," returned George.

"It's too late to cry about it now," said logical Martha. "We can break off some elder bushes and play the sticks are our guns."

"Wouldn't it be a *lot* of fun if we scared up a rabbit, or even a chicken, after we start on our hunt," remarked John.

"No such luck," tittered Martha, gazing everywhere to see if there might be something alive that would do for a make-believe fox.

"There's a clump of alders," George said, as they reached the pasture lot where the horses were kept.

"Yoh don' fear dey is goin' to broncho bust us like th' cow did, eh?" asked Jim, timidly.

"Oh, no!" was Martha's assurance. "These are *old* horses, too feeble and tired to broncho any one."

The alders had been broken off, and

the children were stripping the twigs and leaves from the long branches as they started to cross the lot. The pasture was located in a glade between two knolls, but no sight of the houses of Woodlawn or Vernon Homestead could be had from the pretty valley. The children made sure of this fact before they continued on their fox hunting.

"I fotched a pocketful of corn fer dem. Corn makes 'em come to yo'r han', when yuh wants to cotch 'em," explained Jim, turning a pocket inside out to get at the kernels of chicken corn.

"You're a treasure, Jim," were John's admiring words, as he picked up some of the corn.

"That's right! We never thought of having to catch the horses before we could mount them," said George.

Jim felt very important at such praise, and he gladly gave his three comrades the greatest number of kernels.

One old sorrel horse, very lame in the hind leg, was coming across the grass to see what these early callers wanted in that pasture. Two other horses could be seen at the far side of the lot cropping the dewy grass.

"This sorrel acts as though he would like to try a little trot once more," ventured Martha, churking to the limping horse to coax him nearer to the eager would-be hunters. She didn't know that the sorrel was so deaf that he couldn't hear a steam whistle, even if it blew right at his ear, so she continued to chirrup.

The animal came up fearlessly to the children and poked an inquiring nose at John's palm that held the corn.

"Now John can keep his attention to the corn, while I use this rope and loop it around the nag's neck," said George, quickly removing the coil of washline from about his waist where it had been wound during transit from the house to the pasture.

The old horse stood perfectly still while the rope was tied about his neck, then he found the bountiful giver of the corn had changed his mind about donating more of the delicacy to him.

"Martha, you might get up on his back; John and I will go mount the other horses," advised George.

"What about Jim—does he run on foot with Vulcan, to whip up the fox, or does he ride a horse?" asked John, not ashamed of his ignorance of the way to go fox hunting.

"He's Billy Lee, remember," corrected Martha.

"And he has to go afoot, of course. Jim, you can start across the lot, and Martha will ride after you. John and I will run over and climb up on those other two horses," said George, joyously.

"Dis suah am goin' to be a tip-top game," chuckled Jim, and his comrades agreed heartily with him.

"But how can I climb up on that high back?" now demanded Martha, seeing how slippery the sides of the horse were.

All four sized up the situation, and then the sorrel seemed to answer the problem for them, to the surprise and delight of all four Little Washingtons.

The horse got down upon the ground, and rested upon his haunches for a time.

"Did you ever!" laughed Martha. "He must have been trained to do that, and when he heard me speak, he just got down for me to get upon his back." Then without more loss of time, Martha straddled the old animal's back and took hold of the rope which was about his neck.

"Giddap!" urged she, slapping the sorrel gently upon the side. But the horse never budged.

"Come on there—giddap!" coaxed George, slapping his neck.

Still no action took place with the fox hunter. Then John tried another plan of getting the horse to move. He got back of him and shoved with all his might, at the same time shouting to him to giddap! whoa! back-up! and many other driving terms. Still the horse remained exactly where he had dropped.

"We must all three coax at the same time. John can push, I'll pull on the rope, and Martha must kick with her heels and slap with her hands," advised George.

The three then began these methods, and, suddenly, without other notice, the horse began to roll over and over, having a fine time kicking up his old heels and stretching out his neck.

At the very first roll Martha was thrown off and left sprawling on the grass. George just missed being kicked by the flying heels of the sportive animal; but, in backing quickly, he had tripped over the rope and measured his length on the grass. John and Jim remained with open mouths, gaping at this performance of the sorrel.

"Dat's whad dey do when dey gits colic," was Jim's dire statement.

"Why do they get colic?" asked John, nervously.

"F'om eatin' too much cohn, when dey is on paster feed," was Jim's own interpretation of the malady and its cause.

George and Martha had scrambled to their feet again, and the horse was now through his morning exercises, so he got up and shook himself well. Then he turned and neighed at the Little Washingtons.

"I don't believe he did that on purpose," was Martha's relenting verdict of the rolling.

"Well, then, try his back again," said George. "John and I are going to get the other horses."

"Before you go, boys, you'll have to help boost me up," declared Martha, anxiously.

"Come on, then," retorted George, impatiently. And Martha ran over beside the old horse, and patted him on the neck to let him know she bore him no malice for his trick.

After many slidings and much scrambling Martha reached the top of the sorrel's bare back. Then she took the rope from her brother's hand and was ready to ride cross-country to the fox chase.

"Now you come on, while we two boys hurry and get on our hunting horses," called John, smiling with

pleasure at the way the game was going for them.

Martha tried to drive her steed across
the pasture lot to the place where the
other two animals were to be seen, but
the sorrel paid no attention to her. She
pulled on the rope, and churked, and
giddap-ed until she was hoarse,—not
horse—, still the animal ambled slowly
along the fence-rails beside the road
where the farmer generally passed on
his way to the mill.

Another thing kept Martha from
succeeding in making the horse follow
the hounds to the hunt, and that was
the dreadful way the sorrel's back
heaved and see-sawed. His hind leg
made him limp so badly that his whole
body slumped every time he took a step.
The huntress had all she could do to
remain upon that swaying back, with
no saddle and nothing to hold fast to!

At a certain fence-post the animal
stopped and stretched his head over the
top rail to get at a tendril of green ivy
which had climbed the fence and now

reached up to nothing in particular. The tender sucker of vine was chewed off, and the horse remembered that this was the rail where he had scratched his back so neatly on a former day. He then began to rub his side against the fence, and, in other ways shook and shivered until finally Martha was sliding down his back and had almost reached his tail.

Then the unexpected happened to the sorrel that had just been enjoying life so lazily. A carpenter-bee had constructed her nest in that particular fence-rail, and the horse's way of rolling and pushing the rail angered her. She left her work of lining the nest with pollen for the eggs she had planned to deposit in there, and came out to scold the intruder upon her privacy. She saw a horse, and she knew she could soon drive him from the spot. So she used her weapon to some purpose.

Before Martha had gotten so far back as to make it hopeless for her to cling to the horse, the bee had planted

a stinger directly on the nose of the in-
quisitive animal. In three high leaps
the horse was up and away. Martha
was bounced about on that three-legged
hoppity-limpy gait until she wondered
where she was. She had clung fast to
the rope which still held securely
around the sorrel's neck, but she knew
that it was only a question of seconds
now before she must slide off that uncertain back. All memory of foxes
and hunting trips had vanished from
her mind, and she was concerned only
in reaching the ground without a broken head.

Down to the brook galloped the
limpity animal, and there he thrust his
swollen nose into the cool water. But
where, oh, where was Martha at this
moment?

Why, in a flash, Martha saw the
horse's purpose, and she closed her eyes
and let go the rope. In another moment she was flat upon the grass, her
eyes blinking up at the sun overhead.

After recovering her breath grad-
ually, Martha sat up and called her

friends. What she saw was not to be compared to *her* experience in fox-hunting.

George had just lifted the rope to slip it over the neck of the nearest horse which had been grazing, when the animal stretched forth his mouth and calmly nipped his tormentor on the shoulder. John saw the assault and took to his heels. He ran and ran, shouting to his companions to run for their lives. George, too frightened to run, stood yelling for some one to save him. Jim watched and heard all, his eyes widening and his jaw sagging in dismay.

But the Newfoundland dog had in youth been trained to respond instantly to a call for help, and he felt the old-time zeal to save and succor the needy now driving his stagnated blood through his veins. With a yelp of old-time joy that he might help a hopeless one, he tore the rope from *Billy Lee's* grasp and was away in the direction of George.

Before any one could dream of the

dog's purpose, the big, old Newfoundland had gripped George by the slack seat of his knickerbockers and turned to drag him away from the danger zone, where he had stood yelling for help.

Several yards across the meadow grass the dog had gone with this saved soul, when his unusual spurt of vigor and vim gave out. Then dog and boy rolled together upon the ground, the dog panting like a brokendown engine.

It was about this time that Jim's mammy found her kitchen in such a mess, and the griddle still smoking and burning where it had been left by Washington's cook that morning. Either a band of vagabonds had entered the house and used her kitchen, or those four Little Washingtons were up to some new mischief!

She hastened to granny's room and no Jim was there. She ran upstairs to the children's room—no Martha or George to be seen fast asleep. Then she feared the truth—some new game was on for the day. Where would it end; and would Jim be brought home alive?

Mr. Vernon was an early riser, for he believed that a successful farmer must go to sleep with the birds and get up with them. He was mixing a new kind of ointment to apply to the lame horse's leg, when he heard the wild cries for help. Not knowing how four Little Washingtons played games after the manner of historical readings about the great General, he raced away to the pasture lot. And there he stood and laughed until he was hoarse. Then he began to ask questions, and soon the truth came out. At the same time Mr. Vernon was begged not to share the secret of the fox hunt with any other person; because, thus far, the Little Washingtons had not had success in one of their fine games of farm-life. And they wished to try one or two others before their parents should forbid it.

Laughing as he had not laughed for years, Mr. Vernon promised to keep the fox-chase a secret; then they all started back home. But the farmer began to realize that Pete was right, when he had said that these four Washingtons kept two families as busy as the General-in-chief of the Revolutionary Army had kept the British.

CHAPTER VII

SHALL WE PLAY SHEEP OR SLAVES?

THE unlooked for result of their early fox-chase kept the four Little Washingtons rather quiet for a short time. With these active children a full day was a *long* time, and a half or quarter day was a short time, according to the fun they planned to have.

Mr. Vernon went with them to the barn and helped in making them look presentable once more, because the strenuous time the horses and the dog, to say nothing of the fox (in this case it was a carpenter-bee, Martha said) left them looking rumpled and awry.

"We three will go and sit down quietly under the big pine by the field-path, John, and you go for the book. If Marth or I go and are seen, folks will ask questions—where we've been, and what we were doing," suggested George, after they had thanked Mr. Vernon and were on their way from the barnyard.

So it happened that the Parkes saw their little ones enjoying the farm story of Washington's life, and they refused to believe it possible that these meek-looking children could have created a mess in the kitchen long before any one in the household was astir.

Four Little Washingtons under the pine tree were too engrossed in the farm stories to heed what was said in the house. Martha was reading:

" 'Among Washington's slaves were carpenters, coopers, sawyers, blacksmiths, tanners, spinners, shoemakers, weavers, knitters, and a few to keep his wine-cellars stocked with different kinds of liquor, besides the farm-hands and house-servants.

" 'His woods provided the materials for the carpenters and coopers and the charcoal for fuel; the cattle were raised to keep the larders stocked with meat, and the tanneries supplied with hide. The sheep though not superfine gave enough wool to the weavers; and the cotton and flax fields produced their harvest to employ the spinners and carders as well as the pickers. Carpenters and sawyers had charge of the buildings on the estates; and the coopers kept up the supply of barrels and casks for tobacco, liquor, and salted foods. The tanners, curriers, and shoemakers took charge of the hides from the time they were stripped from the cattle until it came dressed to the persons which would use them—be it in shoes, saddles, or for personal adornment. The spinners, weavers, and knitters were kept busy supplying such a large circle of members with clothing.

"'Besides all these home-products, Washington purchased the fine apparel and luxuries for his family from agents abroad. But it can be seen that so many industries carried on on his own estates would keep a man very busy; and Washington was too thorough in his methods, to permit a paid overseer to take his place in such works.

"'The Revolution took Washington from his interesting farming experiments, and for eight years he gave little time or thought to his estates. Peace at last elected him to the place of honor—the head of a Nation! Finally he returned to his home to continue the pursuits of a country gentleman.'"

George and John had been showing evident signs of boredom, but Martha pretended to ignore them. Then John remarked politely, "Seems to me we waste an awful lot of time every time we read; why can't we find the real games right off, instead of reading and reading things that sound just like lessons?"

"Now that's just the way I feel about it!" declared George, emphatically. Jim, as usual, had nothing to say in such matters.

"The only trouble with you two boys is this: you have been playing war so long that you can't quiet down to play farmer," remarked Martha, with a curl of her lip.

"Maybe so," admitted John, "but here we have a fine big farm, with woods, and a safe pond to play with, and sheep and horses, and everything Washington had at Mount Vernon, so it is a shame to sit and hear baby stuff read to us."

"Good gracious, boys!" exclaimed Martha, impatiently. "We have only been here three days—what do you expect a farmer to do—build a farm, sow the seed, and gather a crop in three days?"

Jim snickered at this, and all eyes looked at him for an explanation. Seeing he was expected to express an opinion he said: " 'Pears to me we-all made a lot of hay in dese free days. Ain't us fished and hunted and trained hosses?"

Three distinct snorts of disdain was Jim's reply, so he sat, after that, with a grim expression on his face, and the decision in his heart that he would *not* be enticed into voicing another idea at these readings, since every one had a different opinion about the stories in the book.

Martha felt that having the book in her possession gave her the privilege of selecting the story. Now she said, "I'm going to read something about the slaves at Mount Vernon; any one that gets bored, can get up and leave, without asking our pardon." As she spoke, she looked straight at George, because she knew he wanted to get the book and read about sheep and Indians. She received no reply to her invitation for some one to get up and go, so she read:

" 'Washington's most famous servant was Thomas Bishop, who was commended to the General by Braddock upon his death-bed. This man-servant remained with Washington until his death. He accompanied his master on his trip to New York and Boston, in 1756, decked out in new liveries of fine cloth, trimmed and faced with scarlet, with a scarlet waistcoat; the hats too were silver-laced, and Bishop must have presented a gorgeous appearance in such raiment.

" 'Bishop was too old to take an active part in the Revolution, so he was left at home to manage the estate.

" 'William Lee, known to all as Billy Lee, was the best known of Washington's slaves on the Mount Vernon estate. He was the General's valet throughout the Revolution, and rode with him at the reviews. It is told of him that he assumed airs because of his personal attendance on the General; and upon one occasion, when Washington and his staff were studying the movements of the British, Billy gathered his valet-companions about him and from a slight prominence near the General's staff calmly surveyed the enemy, Billy gazing intently through a telescope which he had been ordered to take charge of.

" 'Washington smilingly directed the attention of his staff to the men-servants. But at that moment the British, having noticed the group of horsemen standing on the prominence and mistaking them for the General's party, sent a solid shot crashing through the trees. Needless to add that Billy and his friends beat a hasty retreat.

" 'Billy was a good and faithful slave until the year when he and his master were riding to inspect a piece of land. Billy fell and broke his knee-cap, thus crippling himself for life. After this he had to resign from his usual activities, though he insisted upon supervising the duties now assumed by another servant.

" 'Washington's ideas on slavery are interesting. He regarded them as a necessary asset at the time, but he declared that it was all wrong to buy and sell human beings as one would cattle, forgetting that they had hearts and could love even as the whites loved their own. He said he would not own a single slave within a year, were it not for the principle he stood for—that a master should not sell his servants away from the family where they were reared and had established ties of affection.

" 'He wrote: "I wish from my soul that the Legislature of the State could see the policy of a gradual abolition of slavery." His private ideas on this vital subject show that he was in accord with those of our second Great National Father—Abraham Lincoln. However, many said that Washington kept slaves,—why should not other land-owners?

" 'In his will he stated: "Upon the decease of my wife it is my will and desire that all the slaves which I hold *in my own right* shall receive their freedom." He explained that should they be emancipated before her death certain difficulties might arise, on account of the intermixture of the dower negroes with his own slaves; and such an act might cause separation and grief in the negro families.' "

"Seeing that Martha is determined to read stories which we can't play games by, I'm going away to hunt for the sheep we need for a shearing game," announced George, getting up from the grass and walking a few steps from the little group under the pine. He glanced at John and Jim with an inviting expression, but these two members of the Little Washington circle were at a loss what to do: to remain and hear Martha read about slaves, or go with George on the more exciting pastime of hunting sheep for a shearing.

Martha settled the conflict in the souls of her three comrades by resignation with honor and grace. "If you boys will sit down and listen to this one more story, I'll put the book away and go with you to hunt sheep."

John and Jim heaved a sigh of relief, because they had no desire to cause mutiny in the army, and George's abrupt desertion meant mutiny so far as Martha was concerned. Seeing his two companions show signs of remaining for the last story, George leaned against the tree to listen, but he would not weaken so far as to sit down again.

"I just want to read about one of Washington's inventions which was used on his farm," said Martha. "In his day the seed had to be sown by hand and then covered by means of a harrow or hoe. The famous Farmer figured out that a machine would accomplish this work better and faster. So he experimented with a barrel plow, which consisted of a hollow form of barrel mounted upon a plow with wheels. In this barrel were holes, large and small, for the seed to run through. A slide was placed to regulate the amount of seed which the planter wished to drop into the ground; by means of this slide the holes could be left wide open or closed almost entirely.

" 'Washington was proud of his automatic planter and recommended it to his friends. In one letter of description of his seed-barrel, he wrote: "Hang a bag containing a peck of seed to the nail at the right handle of the plow; with a tin cup you can take out enough seed from time to time to keep the barrel supplied."

" 'But he says nothing about the troubles the barrel caused his planters: how it got clogged, or how the leathern belt refused to turn and thus keep the barrel from revolving.' "

George gave vent to an exasperating sigh of impatience, and his sister understood her brother so well that she knew it was high time to end the reading; therefore she closed the book and got up. The three boys seemed only too delighted to have it so.

The comrades started in the direction of the barnyard, hoping to find Mr. Vernon there. If he was found, he might give them some directions to find the sheep they wished to study for a future game. But no one was in sight at the barnyard, nor elsewhere around the farm-land.

"He diden' take the donkey away to-day!" cried Jim, as he peered into the stable and discovered the animal in one of the stalls.

"He said he would allow us to drive him some day, after the cart had been repaired," ventured John, eagerly.

"Maybe the cart *is* repaired," added Martha.

George instantly caught the meaning of these two suggestions and answered,

"I'm going to have a look and see if it is fixed."

"Does yoh know whad ailed it?" asked Jim, wonderingly.

"No; but we can soon find out if it is all right now," retorted George, starting for the carriage house which was divided from the stalls where the horses were kept.

Sheep raising was forgotten for the time, and the Little Washingtons gave their best attention to the matter of the wicker cart. If it was in order, it would certainly prove that the repairs were finished. And Mr. Vernon had plainly said they might take a drive some time when the cart was fixed. Nothing wrong in that, said the children to themselves, to quiet uneasy consciences.

The children, knowing so little of harness and carriages, could find nothing wrong with these.

"You know, Martha just read how Washington taught all kinds of trades to his slaves," remarked John, "and we might play we are those workmen.

One of us can attend to the cart, and play he is the wheelwright; Jim can curry the donkey and get him ready for a drive, so he can be the currier—I s'pose that is what is meant by that name. Another one can see if the harness is good, and that will make a tanner of him, 'cause he is fixing leather, and we know that leather comes from hides."

John's idea was accepted with delight, for now it was all right to harness the donkey to the cart and take a trip —were they not Little Washingtons? —and it was a historical fact that the General-Farmer did all these things on his place, Mount Vernon.

A hasty inspection of the cart, harness and jack by Washington's four eager slaves resulted in a unanimous report that everything was exactly right. Then George glanced warily around the barn and said to Jim, "Go see if any one can be seen about the barnyard, or down the lane."

John went with Jim, because this was a necessary precaution—to be sure no one was in sight to prevent the trip planned. The two scouts then returned and said, "All quiet! No one in sight."

Four perplexed slaves then worried over the many pieces of harness. "Where did that belong? Where can this fit in? What shall we do with this buckle; or with that strap?" asked they of each other. But the answer invariably was: "Fix it where you like, and don't bother with it, if you don't know where it belongs."

Jim had heard Mr. Vernon tell his father, Pete, that the jack's name was "Nero." But neither of the Little Washingtons knew that the name had been given because the animal was so tricky and mean in disposition. He seemed kind and agreeable enough as he stood in the stall and watched proceedings with the harness and cart. Neither were the children aware that the donkey was boarding at Mr. Vernon's farm during the summer, while his owner was abroad.

Having tried to brush down the animal's coat, as Jim thought a good "currier" should do, and seeing an evil gleam shining from the eyes of the donkey, this slave decided that discretion was the wiser part of valor in this instance. So he turned and went back to his comrades, who were handling the parts of the harness.

"Jim," asked George, as the currier-slave joined the tanner, wheelwright, and carpenter, "what is this funny loop of leather meant for?"

"Dat?" explained Jim, groping for some idea which would fit the need. "Why, dat's a head-piece. See: yoh puts it over the animal's head and fas'ens it unner his neck—so." Jim tried to show his friends his method of arranging the complicated object, and they accepted his explanation and never knew the leather had been used for extra strapping for boxes or bundles which had to be carted to town on the gig. It had been used recently and the buckles were not unfastened again; so it was found in its semi-circular shape just as it had been left when the box was removed.

"Take that, John, and put it over the jack's head," ordered George.

"Are we going to call him a jack or a donkey?" asked Martha. "Washington seems to have preferred the jacks, you know."

"Why, I thought we had decided to name him 'Royal Gift' and *he* was a jack," replied George.

"All right, then. I just wanted to know what was what."

Nero, which was the real name of the jack, pretended to be as docile as a lamb, and the Little Washingtons had no difficulty in harnessing him to the cart, in a manner that they thought was right. At least, they used a great deal of harness, never dreaming that there were odds and ends of three or four different sets now wound about the jack's body, or buckled here and there to the cart and to other pieces of leather.

"Are we ready now?" asked Martha, eagerly.

"Where shall we go for this trip: Alexandria or Annapolis?" asked

John, grinning with delight at the excursion promised them.

"Why not start for Philadelphia, or the Federal City?" suggested George.

"We had a trip to Philadelphia, remember? but we never went to the Federal City," said Martha. So Federal City it was to be.

"John and Jim run to the door and scout once more," was George's warning, as he climbed up in the two-wheeled cart.

The boys obeyed, and soon ran back saying the coast was clear. Then John got up beside George, and Jim sat opposite Martha on the back part of the two seats which were placed on the sides of the cart. Nero, or Royal Gift as the Little Washingtons called him, ambled out of the barn in a fine frame of mind; and soon the pleased quartette of travelers giggled and smiled at such great fun.

Contrary to all his former behavior the jack went down the lane at an unusually good pace, and the cart jiggled and rattled at his heels without the slightest hint of trouble to the occupants. There was but one thing to warn the children that there might be a self-willed animal to handle, should there be a difference of opinions between the drivers and the one driven. But they knew nothing of the donkey's stubbornness, and so they were happy.

"Where are we going?" asked Martha, seeing that George held one rein and John the other, and neither one seemed to be using any persuasion to guide the jack.

"We don't know," laughed John.

"Royal Gift knows, and that's all that counts," said George.

As it turned out later, Royal Gift did know! and this was the first time the animal had had his own way since he came to board at Woodlawn Farm. He turned off the good road which ran past the extreme limits of the farm, and kept on running down a poor bit of country lane which bumped the children about like jackstones in a box.

George whoaed in vain—Royal Gift kept on running.

At the top of a long hill the donkey stood gazing around and lifted his nose to sniff the air. The children looked at the distance they had come, and were delighted to think it was so far to travel back again. Up to this time the impromptu harness had held out beautifully; perhaps it was due to the many windings and swaddlings the beast had been given, when the slaves were not certain what to do with the odd ends of leather.

"Shall we turn him around and start back home?" asked John, seeing the countryside was dotted with houses and gardens, instead of the large farms that were about Vernon Homestead and Woodlawn farm.

"Oh, not yet. It's too much fun, to end it so soon," said George.

"But the sun is setting," was his sister's warning. "And it will be suppertime before we can get back to the house."

"Well, let's just go down this hill, and then we'll turn at the bottom and start back for the house," agreed George. But he would now have to reckon with Nero, and not with Royal Gift!

CHAPTER VIII

THE WANDERERS FOUND

AT the bottom of the steep hill, where George planned to turn the donkey's head and start him back home, Nero refused to pay any heed to the tugging on the reins. In fact, the reins were not fastened to any bit, but had been buckled and tied with string to the section of leather straps which had been badly fitted over the donkey's head for a harness.

"We'll make you turn, you balky mule!" threatened John, giving his rein a hard yank. Then to his consternation, the piece of leather came away from the contraption over the animal's head, and he held the other end loosely in his hand.

"Gee! how can we drive him with one rein?" cried George, anxiously.

"You'll have to stop and fix John's leather on again," advised Martha. But saying this was simpler than stopping the jack.

The more the children shouted and coaxed and argued with Nero, the more stubborn he became and the faster he traveled along the bumpy country road.

"If he would only stop long enough to let us tie this dangling rein back on his harness!" wailed John, helplessly holding the strip of leather.

"Where *do* you s'pose he is heading for?" asked Martha, her brow puckered with anxiety.

"How do we know?" snapped George, nervously tugging at the single rein, but without any results whatever.

Jim must have had a deep sense of humor, for now he laughed and said, "Marfa wants to know what dat mule knows; and George gets mad an' says 'how do we know what he knows'—an' we don' know it, dat's shuah; 'kase a mule onny knows his own way an' den he takes it, an' nobuddy kin change him f'om goin' dat way."

George frowned at Jim, then mumbled: "What are you talking about, anyway?"

But an answer was made impossible at this moment. Nero had brought the cart to the crest of a very high hill, and there he made a sharp turn to go in between two stone gate-posts which were the back entrance to a large estate having a rubble-stone wall-fence surrounding the land.

The turn was so sharp, and the harness so weak, that the various loosened ties gave way at the hard tension brought to bear on them. So Nero ran on, but the cart stood still where it had been left when the parting of the ways occurred —the ways of a donkey, and the ways of four Little Washingtons.

While Nero galloped like mad (because he was freed of the swaddling leather and the dragging at his heels of the cart), along the road which passed between the stone posts, the children were huddled in a heap upon the road at the back of the uptilted cart. It had all come upon them so suddenly—this desertion of Nero's—that the two-wheeled cart turned its shafts upward towards the sky, and the tail-board struck the ground. At an angle such as this made, how could a Little Washington remain seated? Well, they couldn't, and all four were tumbled over and over upon the road at the rear step of the vehicle they had thought so trustworthy.

Finally they got up and shook themselves together again. After staring moodily at the dust left by the flying heels of Nero along the driveway of the property before them, and then gazing disconsolately at the far distance where their homes must be, the children turned and looked at each other.

"Now what?" asked John.

"Nuffin, it 'pears to me," said Jim.

"You and your 'nuffin' never get us anywhere!" snapped George, angrily.

"Sometimes Jim is right, like this time," giggled Martha.

"And all you ever do, when we are a thousand miles from supper is to giggle

—if that isn't just like a girl!" retorted her brother, too annoyed to remember that his friends were just as far from supper as he was.

"Even if I am a girl and can giggle instead of quarrel," remarked Martha, still giggling at the situation, "I will suggest that we start in after that mule and make him come back to the cart."

"That's so!" exclaimed John, proving he had not thought of this plan. And George said nothing, but he started for the gate, thus silently confessing his lack of thought-power, too.

The four trudged in past the gate-posts, and followed a long back-road, then finally came in sight of a row of barns, but no residence.

"The house must stand behind those enormous pines," said Martha, nodding in the direction of a small belt of towering trees.

"Yeh," agreed Jim. "Mos' likely dat is a front of it, an' dis end is a back gate." Jim was familiar with the back entrances of the mansions he had visited, so he showed his knowledge now.

"I can't see hide nor hair of that tricky beast," said George, looking around for Nero.

"Isn't it queer how he turned right in here and then ran as though he was glad to meet with friends?" remarked John.

"You never can tell what a donkey thinks," was George's reply.

"That's why he is a donkey," laughed Martha. "And that's why other folks call their friends 'donkeys'—because *they* can't find out what they think."

"Say, I see dat mule a-gallopin' across th' grass, goin' f'om th' stables up to th' house,—see?" called Jim, pointing in the direction he described.

"Sure enough! *Now* where is he bound for?" gasped John.

"We'll have to chase him—even if he takes us to the parlor," said Martha, starting off across the grass to follow Nero.

It took some time to cross the vast stretch of lawn, and, when the four children got to the thick growth of pines, they found Jim's idea was right—the trees formed a heavy screen between the mansion and the stables. And such a fine house as it was!

"Did you ever!" exclaimed Martha, staring at the imposing place. "It's bigger'n our house down South."

"But look,—every window closed in by the shutters, and the doors boarded up. It looks as though the place was vacant," said John.

"So it is! But where did that donkey go?" muttered George.

"Listen! I hear the sound of hoofs echoing down that way," called Martha, running to the other side of the house to verify her words. "Yes— there he goes, the rascal!"

The boys had followed Martha, and now they saw Nero galloping back to the barns. Without waiting to give another look at the house the children ran after the only hope they had of reaching Woodlawn that night. But theirs was a "Lost Hope" it seems.

Reaching the stables in a hot and breathless condition, the four comrades found the place barred and boarded up even as the mansion had been. But they also found that the donkey could not have found a way inside this stable. They turned to leave the barnyard, and then caught sight of Nero running along the back road by which he had entered the premises.

"Quick! quick!" warned Martha, racing away in the direction the donkey had taken. "We've got to catch him before he starts home, or we'll have to walk."

This was an incentive which gave spurs to the boys' feet, and away went the four friends, running as for a medal. But it proved a hopeless race, because Nero outdistanced them without a backward glance.

When the Little Washingtons reached the upturned cart once more, Nero was halfway down the long-steep hill. He kept on going and soon reached the foot, where he had the meanness to stop and turn and look back at those he had left behind him.

"Why! you horrid little thing, you!" shouted Martha, shaking her fist at him. As though this roused Nero's laughter,

even as another Nero would laugh
when his victims burned or begged for
mercy, he opened his mouth and
sounded a loud "Hee-haw! hee-haw!"
Then he resumed his gallop for Woodlawn Farm.

"What shall we do,—miles from
home, and no one apt to pass along this
dreadful country road," complained
George.

"There isn't room in the cart for us
to sleep there," said John, sizing up the
cramped accommodations for a night.

"We can crawl under those pines
and sleep on the thick bed of needles,
which always carpet the ground under
such old trees," suggested Martha,
looking back at the strip of trees near
the house.

"We might miss some one driving
past here," objected George.

"Then one ought to remain here,
while the others rest there," responded
Martha. "I see it will be hard to
choose one to remain—you all want to
go with the majority, don't you?"

"Well," explained George, placing

his hands over an empty stomach, "We've had a dreadful day of it, Marth. Such a poor breakfast at daybreak, and then not much lunch this noon, and no supper at all to-night! If we got to sleep, we might forget our hunger."

"We have to follow the old way of deciding, I see," was Martha's reply. "Draw lots for the one who has to sit in the cart and call any one that passes here. The rest can go and sleep yonder."

Four blades of grass were gathered, and Jim was chosen the holder. He always was holder because his friends had perfect faith in his honesty. He would not permit his hands to slide *the least bit,* to move a blade of grass up or down—no, not even in times when he wanted to go with the others, and not remain behind all alone on a dark country road, in a place where wolves and foxes might catch him!

The drawing of the lot of that one who must summon all the brave Washington spirit to his side for the night now began. Before the blades had been chosen, however, the welcome sound of a horse's hoofs reached the weary wanderers, and they ran to the road which forked away around the scrub pines. There they saw an angel of mercy approaching—but the angel was on horseback!

The rider rode up to the crest-fallen children and gazed at them in astonishment. Then he saw the cart and fallen harness, and thought he understood the situation.

"You poor children! Where did the Shetland go after he broke away?" asked the rider.

"It wasn't a Shetland," explained George viciously, as he thought of that hee-haw the donkey sent them from the foot of the hill. "He was the meanest little jack that you ever saw!"

The man laughed heartily, and then said, "I only knew of one mean donkey, and that was Nero. But he isn't here any more."

"Who is Nero? Where did he live?" asked Martha, light breaking upon her clouded mind.

"He lived in there," explained the rider, pointing his whip in the direction of the stables where the donkey had raced after leaving the children in the cart outside the gate. "But his owners are away this year, so Nero went to board with Farmer Vernon."

"W-h-y, Vernon's where we live!" exclaimed George, and Martha nodded her head gladly. Here was help for them!

"Is that so! Well, Vernon told me he had a ready-made little family for this summer, and I see he is right. But let me warn you not to trust Nero's promises again. He will fail you at the most important times." The man chuckled as he advised the four children.

"Then his name isn't Royal Gift after this. He can keep the name of Nero—it suits him!" declared Martha.

The rider knew nothing of the Washington games, and he had no clew to a name of Royal Gift for a donkey, so he merely smiled. Then he said: "What shall you do now—with your

locomotive gone home, and no other
way to be found of hitching power to
that cart?"

Even while the man was speaking a
daring plan entered Martha's brain.
Why not! It seemed perfectly good,
and might be tried.

"We have lots of harness there," suggested she, meaningly.

"So I see," returned the man, but he
had not understood her.

"In fact, there would be enough harness to hitch up the cart to a *big* horse,
you know. I think there would be
plenty, to allow the cart to be pulled
on behind a regular horse, while the
man rode on its back," hinted Martha
broadly. In fact, so broadly that all
the children saw her point. The man
laughed uproariously.

"How would Centaur act if he had
to have the cart bumping at his nervous
heels? And how would he hold back
the precious freight inside the cart, on
these steep hills with no brake to stop
the two wheels from running away
from me?" As though the horse un-

derstood his master's speech, he began to prance and dance around nervously.

"Maybe you can suggest a way to help us get home,—or we shall have to finish our drawing of the lot for one to sit here all night, while the rest of us go over to sleep under those pines." Martha threw every bit of persuasive art into her words, and a far stonier heart than the one owned by this rider would have melted at the pitiful picture she portrayed with the tones of her voice.

"I hear you have a car at the Homestead. Why not let me race across country and tell the man to come and get you?" said he.

"That would be fine—but how about the cart?" said John.

"You can carry the harness back in the car, but no one will take the cart. No one ever comes this way, only the family living in that house and my family. We live on the other knoll, and we only ride this way when we wish to take a long canter."

The Little Washingtons watched

their friend ride away in the direction previously taken by Nero, then they sat down upon the harness to wait for the coming of Pete with the car.

"Do you know," ventured John, thoughtfully, "we never saw a single sheep all the way across this country."

"And there were plenty of hills where they might graze," added George.

"Maybe there are no sheep in Vermont," returned John.

"If we want to shear them for a game, I think we will have to use goats," suggested Martha, seriously.

"Or—you know what I said one time!" hinted George.

"You mean—black wool?" giggled Martha.

Jim was not aware of their hints or meanings, so he had no qualms about losing his hair. Perhaps many other games could be played before the plan of shearing a sheep would come to mind again.

"I think we ought to ask Farmer Vernon to tell us new stories of his ancestor's part in the Revolution," remarked John, after a silence in which all four sat thinking over the past few days.

"I agree with John," said George. "Such games seem more fun than the kind we have had to read out of Washington's book on farming."

"I vote that we put that dry book up on a shelf, and let Mr. Vernon supply us with his kind of games," added Martha.

"Yoh better not shelf dat book," warned Jim, wisely. "Yo'r mammy will fin' it an' know you ain't takin' no part in Washerton's fahm life. Dis is a Wermont fahm, and folks think us-all ought to stick to fahmin'. We kin *play* read dat book, but when we *do* play it kin be the sort of fahm-game we get from Mr. Wernon—see?"

Yes, the Little Washingtons saw!

Also they soon saw an automobile climbing the long hill which led to the crest, where they were perched upon the harness resting their weary backs against the wheel of the cart.

"Say!" bawled the welcome voice of

Pete, as he stopped the car beside the up-turned cart. "How did you rascals get here?"

"We were not the rascals—Nero was it!" declared Martha. "Pete, do you know, that mule wouldn't turn one bit along the road we wanted him to follow? He just raced and raced the way he set his heart on coming, and we had to sit in that cart and let him bring us here."

"I hope you don't think we *wanted* to come so far?" now demanded George, surprised at such an error in Pete's mind.

"No sir-ee!" added John, emphatically. "Jim and me were doing everything to stop Nero, but he just wouldn't be stopped. I tried so hard that the rein broke off short at his head."

Pete had not stopped laughing, and now at these explanations, he tried to say between laughs: "Nero came home just before I left the place, and not a sign of harness could we find. We thought you four had taken him out for a drive,—seeing the cart and three sets of harness were gone, too. Then when we saw the donkey trot in, worn out and ready to drop, Mr. Vernon said he was sure the rascal had gone home for a visit, but had to come back when he found the place closed for the season. No one dreamed that Nero had brought you so far from home only to play this trick on you."

On the drive back to Woodlawn the children explained to Pete just why they went for the drive.

"We want to locate some sheep, Pete, because we really do not care to hurt Jim's feelings by *not* using sheep wool, you see," explained George.

"Yes, Pete. But we have come to the conclusion that sheep do not thrive in Vermont, any more than they did on Washington's Mount Vernon farm," added Martha.

"What can you ever want sheep for?" asked Pete, astonished.

"Oh, just for another new game," explained John, casually.

"Well, better stop any new games afore you start 'em, is my advice," said

Pete. But the children knew that Pete had no sense of the fun to be had in playing Little Washingtons.

Perhaps poor Jim would have been the "black sheep," and have lost his wool, had it not been for the diverting news that awaited the children at their homecoming.

"George, Martha!" exclaimed Mrs. Parke, when she heard the noisy entrance of the four patriots, "Come here and listen to the reading of this telegram from Philadelphia."

"From Philadelphia?" shouted George, in a tremor of excitement, as he instantly remembered the fierce battle with the wild street urchins, which the Quaker City cousins and Martha and he had won, in the backyard of that exclusive Colonial home.

"Oh! can it be that our cousins are coming here to visit us?" cried Martha, clasping her hands in the hope of such a joy.

"That all depends," was Mr. Parke's reply, with a serious glance at each of the four heroes of the American Army.

"It all depends on you children," added Mrs. Parke meaningly. "If there are to be any such battle scenes as you provided for us in Philadelphia at the time of our visit there, it would be wise to wire back for your uncle and aunt to come here without the children. Grandma has offered to take them with her in the country for the time being."

"Oh, no!" exclaimed the Little Washingtons in a chorus. "Do have them visit us here."

"If we do so, what guarantee can you give us that the State of Vermont will not become the battlefield of Bunker Hill?" laughed Mr. Graham.

"Oh!" instantly retorted Martha, giving her brother a sly dig in the ribs to insure his silence, "We will promise on our honor that this will not happen— only, please, have our cousins visit us this summer."

And George added pathetically: "Who knows when we all will ever have such a farm and such a quiet life again!"

An encouraging laugh greeted this

remark, and it was quickly agreed that the Philadelphia cousins might come.

Later Martha explained to her three confederates: "You know, it is simply impossible for us to fight any Bunker Hill battle in Vermont, where we cannot truly find such a place. So I was really safe in promising Daddy and the others our honor in not moving that Hill from Massachusetts into Vermont."

"All the same, Marth," retorted John, "we must stick to the spirit as well as to the letter of the law—I heard my mother say so to your mother."

"Huh, that will be easy enough to do," returned George. "We might postpone playing any more wars or Washington's farm life, and try some of his experiences with house parties."

"Yes! yes!" agreed the three eager hearers. "We will now start our games about the general's entertainments. Our cousins will be the guests."

And so it happened that the Little Washingtons' Parties followed.

THE END

THE LITTLE WASHINGTONS SERIES

By LILLIAN ELIZABETH ROY

**Handsomely Bound. Colored Wrappers. Illustrated.
For Children 6 to 12 Years**

This series presents early American history in a manner that impresses the young readers. George and Martha Washington Parke, two young descendants of the famous General Washington, follow in play, the life of the great American.

THE LITTLE WASHINGTONS

Their thrilling battles and expeditions generally end in "punishment" lessons read by Mrs. Parke from the "Life of Washington." The culprits listen intently, for this reading generally gives them new ideas for further games of Indian warfare and Colonists battles.

THE LITTLE WASHINGTONS' RELATIVES

The Davis children visit the Parke home and join zealously in the games of playing George Washington. So zealously, in fact, that little Jim almost loses his scalp.

THE LITTLE WASHINGTONS' TRAVELS

The children wage a fierce battle upon the roof of a hotel in New York City. Then, visiting the Davis home in Philadelphia, the patriotic Washingtons vanquish the Hessians on a battle-field in the empty lot back of the Davis property.

THE LITTLE WASHINGTONS AT SCHOOL

After the school-house battle the Washingtons discover a band of gypsies camping near their homes and incidentally they recover a stolen horse which the gypsies had taken from a farmer.

THE LITTLE WASHINGTONS' HOLIDAYS

They spend a pleasant summer on adjoining farms in Vermont. During a voyage they try to capture a "frigate" but little Jim is caught and about to be punished by the Captain when his confederates save him.

THE LITTLE WASHINGTONS; FARMERS

Nero, the donkey, had never heard of George Washington, and so the game the children had planned after reading the story of the General's life on his farm turned out to be quite a different game altogether.

GROSSET & DUNLAP, *Publishers*, NEW YORK

LITTLE JOURNEYS TO HAPPY-LAND

By DAVID CORY

Profusely Illustrated. Individual Colored Wrappers.

Printed in large type—easy to read.
For children from 6 to 8 years.

A new series of exciting adventures by the author of the LITTLE JACK RABBIT books. This series is unique in that it deals with unusual and exciting adventures on land and sea and in the air.

THE CRUISE OF THE NOAH'S ARK
This is a good rainy day story. On just such a day Mr. Noah invites Marjorie to go for a trip in Noah's Ark. She gets aboard just in time and away it floats out into the big wide world.

THE MAGIC SOAP BUBBLE
The king of the gnomes has a magic pipe with which he blows a wonderful bubble and taking Ed. with him they both have a delightful time in Gnomeland.

THE ICEBERG EXPRESS
The Mermaid's magic comb changes little Mary Louise into a mermaid. The Polar Bear Porter on the Iceberg Express invites her to take a trip with him and away they go.

THE WIND WAGON
Little Hero stepped aboard the Wind Wagon and started on a journey to many wonderful places and had a delightful time.

THE MAGIC UMBRELLA
A little old man gave Jimmy the Magic Umbrella which took him to Happyland, where he had many adventures.

GROSSET & DUNLAP, Publishers, NEW YORK

TUCK-ME-IN TALES

(Trademark Registered)

By ARTHUR SCOTT BAILEY

AUTHOR OF THE

SLEEPY-TIME TALES and SLUMBER-TOWN TALES

Colored Wrappers and Illustrations Drawn by HARRY L. SMITH

A delightful and unusual series of bird and insect stories for boys and girls from three to eight years old, or thereabouts.

THE TALE OF JOLLY ROBIN

THE TALE OF OLD MR. CROW

THE TALE OF SOLOMON OWL

THE TALE OF JASPER JAY

THE TALE OF RUSTY WREN

THE TALE OF DADDY LONG-LEGS

THE TALE OF KIDDIE KATYDID

THE TALE OF BETSY BUTTERFLY

THE TALE OF BUSTER BUMBLEBEE

THE TALE OF FREDDIE FIREFLY

THE TALE OF BOBBIE BOBOLINK

THE TALE OF CHIRPY CRICKET

THE TALE OF MRS. LADYBUG

THE TALE OF REDDY WOODPECKER

THE TALE OF GRANDMA GOOSE

GROSSET & DUNLAP, *Publishers*, NEW YORK